THE TRUTH CHRONICLES

Book 2: THE CONTEST

TIM CHAFFEY &
JOE WESTBROOK

ILLUSTRATED BY
MELISSA "INKHANA" MATHIS

Risen Books
Richmond, Kentucky

2019

The Truth Chronicles: The Contest
Copyright © 2010 by Tim Chaffey & Joe Westbrook.
All rights reserved.
Second Printing, 2019

Edited by Reagen Reed
Illustrated by Melissa "Inkhana" Mathis

www.RisenBooks.com
Risen Books is an imprint of Risen Ministries, LLC
Richmond, Kentucky

ISBN-13: 978-0-9840931-0-6
ISBN-10: 0-9840931-0-9

Printed in the United States of America

For Kayla and Judah

PROLOGUE

Jax Thompson screeched the car to a halt in his driveway, his eyes fixed on the unfamiliar black sedan parked in front of the garage. His mind raced furiously over what his mother had said on the phone just a few minutes earlier: "Just come home, now. It's about your father." *What's going on? Dad's been dead for more than three years.* After turning the car off, he jumped out the driver's door and slammed it behind him.

An intimidating man in a black suit climbed out of the sedan and blocked his path to the house. "You must be Jax," he said with an unconvincing smile before another man appeared on the driver's side.

Is this the reason Mom sounded so frantic? Jax glared at the man who spoke to him. "Yeah, I'm Jax. Who are you?"

He flashed a badge and said, "I'm Special Agent Kimball and this is Special Agent Johnson. We're conducting an investigation into the destruction of the lab where your father worked."

Jax heard his front door open and turned to see his mom step out.

"Jax, come inside. You don't have to talk to them." She shifted her gaze to Agent Kimball, and her voice turned cold. "I told you I wanted you to leave before my son came home."

"We're sorry Mrs. Thompson," Kimball said. "We were just leaving when he pulled up and thought we might as well ask him a few questions."

"There's nothing else he can tell you. Jax, come inside."

Kimball stepped to the side. "We'll keep you posted if we make any progress."

Jax hurried up the steps to the door, pausing to look into his mother's tense face. "Mom, what's going on?"

"I'll tell you in a minute," she said without taking her eyes off the agents in the driveway.

Frowning, Jax squeezed past her and sat on a couch in the living room. His mom continued her watch at the door until the agents drove away. When she finally turned, all the fire had gone out of her.

Jax tried to be patient as she slunk into her overstuffed chair, but his emotions were still frayed. Not twenty minutes ago the girl of his dreams had shot him down because he didn't believe in her God. And now this. He couldn't wait. "Mom?"

She looked up at him and wiped tears from her eyes. "I'm sorry I missed the science fair, but those men showed up right when I was preparing to leave."

"What did they want?"

She shook her head. "Oh honey, I don't know how to tell you this." She looked at the ceiling and took a deep breath. "They said that the investigation is being re-opened and they have reason to think the explosion wasn't an accident, but was an inside job."

"An inside job?"

"Your dad's security code was the only one activated at the time. They...they suggested that he was involved in some sort of break-in attempt to steal his technology."

Jax shot to his feet. "What? That's impossible. Dad would never have done that."

She sniffled as she stood and hugged him. "I know, Jax. I know."

ONE

Micky pushed a few strands of hair from her face, leaned close to JT, and whispered, "I can't believe this is happening."

JT smiled, all the while keeping her eyes on the reporters. The girls sat together at a table full of microphones in the school gymnasium. JT tried to focus on the questions.

"Are you saying you've actually managed to counter gravity?" a reporter from the *Silicon Valley Times* asked.

Micky adjusted her sleeve. "Well, as we explained—"

"Where is your project so we can see it in action?" asked a journalist from a national morning news program.

"Unfortunately some of our classmates—"

"How does the device work?"

"Where will you go with the scholarship?"

JT leaned close to the mics. "As Micky was trying to say—"

"Has the government contacted you about this yet?"

"When can we expect flying cars?"

Mr. Li stepped up to the table and put a hand on JT's shoulder. "Ladies and gentlemen. If you could ask your questions one at a time and wait until the girls have answered before asking more, we can move this along more smoothly. Now, why don't we start with the question of how the device works?"

Micky cleared her throat. "Basically what we've done is design an emitter that puts out an electromagnetic field. The strength of the field is determined by the size of the emitter as well as the energy source. Using a wall outlet with our device proved to be too powerful, but regular batteries did the trick. So, in answer to the question about overcoming gravity, yes, we have succeeded."

"Does the device have a name?" asked the *Times* reporter.

"At the moment, not really. Some of our classmates have taken to calling it the 'floating bear.'"

"And can we see this 'floating bear'?"

"Um, sadly, no," JT said.

"What do you mean, 'No'?" asked Martin Knutson, a young, sharply dressed correspondent from Six O'clock Action News.

"Two of the guys in our class made a disintegration ray gun, and they smoked our project," Micky said.

This elicited a few chuckles from the crowd.

"So we've got hovering toys and ray guns," Knutson said. "I know this school has a good reputation, but this sounds like science fiction to me. Are you just making all of this up to get attention?"

"No way," Micky said. "We really did make

that toy hover above the table. Why else would the judges have given us first place last night?"

"Maybe they're in on the whole thing, too," said Knutson.

JT opened her mouth to object, but a short, overweight reporter with greasy black hair picked up Knutson's line of questioning and overrode her. "Mr. Li, are you guys just trying to get into the news again after losing your number one science school ranking last year?"

JT blinked back the moisture in her eyes and noticed Micky's face reddening.

Mr. Li stepped forward again to speak into the microphone. "Are you seriously accusing us of lying? Everyone knows we have a great science school. That's why we routinely have judges from Sandia and MIT here. Do you really think they're in on it, too? We don't need to make stuff up to get attention. These girls worked hard for their award and you are accusing them of fraud. You should apologize immediately."

But Knutson wasn't finished lambasting them yet. "If you're telling us the truth, then why don't you just produce that ray gun?"

"We can't," Mr. Li said. "It shattered last night when it hit the floor during the mishap."

"Well that's convenient," said the overweight man. "Maybe they could repair it at Area 51."

Someone in the back of the group shouted,

"Or maybe Atlantis." The entire group of reporters started laughing.

Mr. Li leaned over the microphone again. "This interview is over. Ladies, please follow me."

JT was all too ready to leave, and Micky was fast on her heels. As they followed Mr. Li to the exit, the reporters shouted ridiculous questions after them.

JT fought back tears as Mr. Li led them down the hall. *How could they not believe us? It isn't fair.*

When they reached the parking lot, Mr. Li turned and rubbed the back of his neck. "I'm so sorry this turned out the way it did."

"Why don't they believe us?" JT asked. "We don't have any reason to lie about it."

Shrugging, Mr. Li shook his head. "Reporters are typically pretty skeptical of stuff like this. It's their job to be inquisitive and they all get pretty competitive knowing that scandal usually sells better than success. I guess sometimes they forget there are real people involved. I'm really sorry." Mr. Li opened the door to his car.

"We can prove it," Micky said.

JT shot a quick glance at Micky and elbowed her in the side. "You promised."

Micky chewed her bottom lip and sighed. "Sorry, JT." She looked at Mr. Li. "We have four bigger devices that can make a whole car hover."

JT put her hands on her hips. "Micky."

Mr. Li stood with his right foot in the car, stunned. "What are you talking about?"

"I said I'm sorry, but I can't keep it a secret. Not after those reporters were making fun of us."

Mr. Li stood up straight. "Wait. Are you saying that you made more of those devices?"

"Yeah," Micky said. "They're on Jax's time machine right now."

"That's incredible. I can't wait to see them. In fact, I'm heading over to his house around 11:30 to grade their project. Would you like to meet me there? I'm sure Jax wouldn't mind."

"I'd like to, but I'm taking my driver's test today," Micky said.

JT thought of her conversation with Jax the night before and wondered if she would be welcome at his house. Her stomach clenched as she remembered how hurt he'd been when she told him she couldn't date him. Shaking her head, she said, "I'd like to go too, but right now isn't a good time. Thanks for the offer."

"Sure. See you in class Monday."

JT waved as Mr. Li got into his car and left the parking lot. Micky hopped onto her bike and looked at JT. "I hope this is the last time I have to ride my bike home from school. See ya."

"Yeah, later."

JT sat down on a bench and texted her mother. "We're done."

As she waited for a ride, her thoughts turned to the press conference. *How could they be so rude? I wish we could have showed them that we really were successful.* She wiped her eyes with the back of her hand and cut off a small sob.

Her mother arrived a few minutes later, and she got into the car without saying a word.

"What's the matter, honey?" Mrs. Bankers asked.

"It wasn't good, Mom. No one believed that we actually did it. They didn't even believe Mr. Li." A tear fell from her eye, and her mom gave her a one-armed hug.

"I'm sorry, sweetie. I know you guys put a lot of work into that project, and it's frustrating to have so many people doubting you. I don't know why things happened this way, but God can work through it to strengthen you."

"Yeah, I know." She managed a weak smile. "It's just a lot to take, especially after the argument with Jax last night. He was so upset."

"Well, your father and I are both very happy that you stuck with your convictions. And I'm sure God is pleased that you chose His way instead of following your feelings. We can't force Jax to believe, but we can keep praying for him."

JT's smile brightened a little. *I'm sure he won't stay mad for long.*

"Thanks, Mom."

"Yeah, that should work," Jax said to himself as he drew out some rough sketches. He had been trying to think of ways to reconfigure the girls' technology so that it could be controlled inside the time machine. Their previous trip through time had been dangerous enough. They were chased by a hungry allosaurus, and the girls needed to hang out the back doors of a car flying thirty feet in the air to manually control the rear repulsors. As far as he was concerned, that was a risk he didn't want to repeat.

Looking at the clock, he decided to try calling Izzy again. Mr. Li would be there any minute to grade their project, which they had decided not to enter in the science fair because of the top-secret power source they had commandeered from Jax's dad's prototypes.

The phone rang twice before he heard, "Hi, this is Izzy. Leave your name and number—"

Jax hung up and then slammed his free hand on the desk. *Where could he be? It's almost 11:30.*

"Are you okay in there?" his mother asked from the hallway.

"Yeah, I'm just frustrated. I can't get a hold of Izzy and he's supposed to be here by the time Mr. Li shows up."

Just then the doorbell rang. "That could be Izzy now," she said.

Jax jumped up. "I'll get it." He hurried to the

front door and opened it. "Oh, hi, Mr. Li."

Mr. Li looked the same as he did every day, except for the fact that he wasn't wearing his sport coat. *I wonder if Mr. Li wears the same outfit every day or if he just happens to have a dozen khaki dress pants, white shirts, and skinny black ties.* "Thanks again for coming over to do this. Izzy and I really appreciate it."

"You're very welcome. Speaking of Isaiah, is he inside?"

"No, I can't get a hold of him. I don't know why he's not here."

"I see. Well, I suppose I can look over your project without him."

"Yeah, I just wish he were here to explain the software to you. Can you meet me by the garage door? I'll go open it up." Jax walked into the garage from the kitchen and opened the large door. Mr. Li stepped in, and Jax led him through to a smaller door.

"My dad built the addition to make a lab so he could sometimes work at home. Izzy and I have been using it to do our work now." He opened the door and flipped on the light switch. A smile crossed his lips when Mr. Li whistled in amazement.

"This is quite the setup. It doesn't look quite so big from the outside."

"Well, here it is," Jax said as he walked to the

time machine and patted the hood a couple of times. "Don't let the car fool you. It's not in great shape, but it runs and it was all we could afford."

"Where should I start?"

"Why don't you go around to the passenger side and climb in? I'll jump in the other side and explain everything."

Mr. Li looked impressed when he opened the passenger door. Even from the outside, it was easy to see the rebuilt dashboard full of gauges, switches, lights, and a mounted laptop. A massive conduit full of cables ran across the roof of the car from the top of the windshield all the way back to the trunk.

As Jax booted up the laptop, he explained how he and Izzy had transformed the car as well as the complex theories about time travel. Pulling up the program, he went through as much of the programming as he could without Izzy there, then demonstrated how they selected their destination.

Next he opened the trunk. "So there it is." He pointed at a foot-long cylinder about six inches in diameter. "That's the Space-Time Generator, which is what makes time travel possible. And this right here," Jax said as he picked up a small cube and handed it to his teacher, "is my dad's solar cell that we told you about."

Mr. Li turned the battery in his hand as he studied it. "And this little thing powers the whole car? You know, your dad was really doing ground-breaking work. Thanks for trusting me with this. I understand why you couldn't enter it in the science fair, and I promise to keep it secret."

"Thank you. I really appreciate that."

"So," Mr. Li said as he crossed his arms and smiled. "Just how do you intend to prove to me that this thing actually travels through time?"

Jax looked away. "Uh, well, Izzy and I agreed that we wouldn't take a trip without the other person, so I can't demonstrate it without him."

Mr. Li nodded slowly, a mixture of skepticism and disappointment on his face. "Listen, I want to believe you. I really do. You certainly have some high tech stuff here, but this whole idea is still hard to accept without tangible proof."

"But it really does work."

"I'm sorry, Jax. It's obvious you guys did a lot of work on the car, and I saw your paperwork, but you're claiming to have done something that no one in the history of the world has accomplished before. I can't give you a top score unless you demonstrate it."

How can I prove it? "Izzy will die if he loses his 4.0. What if I told you all about our trip? Would that count?"

"Not unless you can truly convince me."

"Okay, here goes." Jax spent the next ten minutes explaining the wild adventure he'd had with

Izzy, JT, and Micky. He stretched his memory to recall every detail, from the smell of the allosaurus' breath as it glared down at him from the cliff to the shape of the leaves on Izzy's tree.

When he finished, Mr. Li asked, "So you're telling me that they will all support your story?"

"They should. They were there."

"Alright, I'll make my assessment after talking to each of them on Monday. I need to have my grades turned in by the end of the day. But without tangible proof I think the best I could give you guys is a *B*. Even though this is a big assignment, you will probably still have an *A* for the semester."

He stepped out of the car. "Oh, one other thing. Micky mentioned the hover technology that she and JT had made. Can I see that?"

"Sure, they're underneath the car."

Mr. Li examined the devices for a few moments before Jax asked, "You wanna see 'em in action?"

Flashing Jax a grin, Mr. Li said, "You know I would."

"I thought you'd say that." Jax turned the key to engage the battery. He reached across the passenger seat and nudged the sliding levels up. The car rose slightly. "It will go about forty feet up."

Mr. Li whistled. "Wow. That really is amazing."

Jax brought the car back to the ground, turned off the power, and got out. "Yeah, it's pretty awesome, but they also run off the solar cell, so you can't say anything about these, either."

"I understand that it's confidential, but you sure aren't making my job easy. Thanks for showing me these things and for all your work on the project." He turned to walk out the door. "I'll see you on Monday."

"Alright, sounds good. See ya."

Jax followed him to the door. "It really does work."

He turned, smiled, and then waved before walking the rest of the way to his car.

As soon as he pulled away from the driveway, Izzy raced up the sidewalk from the other direction on his bicycle. "Was that Mr. Li?"

"Yeah. I couldn't prove to him the machine works without you and we lost points. Where were you?"

"Sorry." Izzy set his bike down and kicked at the ground. "My dad stopped over. And you know how that usually turns out."

Jax's irritation lessened at the mention of Izzy's dad. He put a hand on his friend's shoulder. "Sorry, man." Jax turned back to the garage. "Well, the good news is that if you and the girls corroborate my story, we'll get a B. Thanks to my quick thinking, you'll still get an A for the semester."

"In that case," Izzy said, following Jax to the garage lab, "maybe it's better this way."

"How's that?"

"We've already seen how quickly things can go wrong. The more I think about it, the more I realize how easily we could ruin the present."

Jax picked up a spool of wire and pretended to examine it. Izzy's words brought a tight knot of foreboding to his stomach, but they didn't change his mind. He had a plan. There was something he felt he had to do, and Izzy wasn't going to like it.

TWO

"Are you sure the girls are going to be okay with this?" Izzy asked Jax as he mounted a joystick near the middle of the time machine's cluttered dashboard.

"They aren't going to care," Jax said around the screwdriver in his mouth. He was underneath the car trying to hook the rear repulsors to the joystick. "Besides, they can't use 'em anyway—not without my power supply."

After three hours of work, the modifications were almost complete. Jax was anxious to finish and put his plan into action, though he wasn't looking forward to telling Izzy about it.

"Hello. Earth to Jax."

"Huh?"

"I asked how things went with JT last night."

Jax gave a noncommittal grunt.

"Oh, come on. You made your move last night, didn't you?"

"There's nothing between us. And I'm pretty sure there never will be."

"Why not?" Izzy bent down and smiled at Jax. "I know you like her."

He knew that he couldn't hide his feelings about JT from Izzy. Jax let his hands fall to the floor and stared into space. "That's not the point. Of course I like her. But she's not willing to give me another shot. Apparently, I'm not good enough for her since I don't let the words of an ancient book rule my life." He regretted saying the words as soon as they came out; he didn't like bad-mouthing JT.

"You're saying that she won't go out with you because of her religion?"

"Pretty much. She told me that she can't date anyone that doesn't believe in her view of God."

After an awkward silence, Izzy said, "Man, I always thought JT was different. I mean, I knew she was religious, but I had no idea she was so intolerant. She shouldn't care what you believe, as long as you aren't hurting anybody."

Something about that didn't seem quite right, but Jax couldn't pinpoint it. Shaking it off, he asked, "So is it true that you and Micky agreed to go to her youth group this week?"

"Yeah, I guess so. I think she won the little debate we were having, so we agreed to go with her. Are you going?"

"She invited me, and since you guys are, I probably will." After a couple moments of silence, Jax slid himself out from under the car. "There it is. I think I've got it. Did you get those levels moved over, too?"

"Yep, it's all set."

"Good. Let's try it out." Izzy moved the joystick around while Jax checked to see how each repulsor responded. "They all look good." Jax stood and climbed in the driver's seat. "Buckle up. Time for another trip."

Izzy raised his eyebrows. "What? Right now? Where are we going?"

"Back to the night my dad's lab exploded."

Izzy crossed his arms and shook his head.

"Just hear me out. Last night, when I got home, there were two government agents here. They had been talking to my mom for over four hours trying to get information out of her. They seem to think that the explosion wasn't an accident, but that my dad was in on some sort of break-in gone wrong. I'm going to prove his innocence."

"But Jax, you can't go back and change the past. It could create one of those space-time paradoxes. If you warn him, then we would have never built the time machine to go back and warn him. Who knows what would happen?"

"We're not going to change anything about that night. All I'm going to do is record the break-in." Jax pointed to his video camera bag sitting in the back seat of the time machine.

"What will that prove? I'm sure they've already seen video footage from the security cameras."

"We were told that all the cameras were destroyed in the blast. There's a hotel near the parking lot with windows on each level of the stairwell. So we'll just hover and make it look like it came from someone in the hotel. Maybe we'll be able to get a good enough shot for the authorities to figure out who caused the explosion."

Izzy's expression wavered. "But even if we succeed, we can't just give the footage to some cop."

Shaking his head, Jax said, "It's okay. I've already thought about it. I'll send the memory card anonymously to the authorities. And we'll make sure that there are no fingerprints on it or the package that we send." He put a hand on his friend's shoulder. "Please, Iz. I just want to clear my dad's name."

Izzy looked out his window and scratched his head. "Okay, I'm in." He turned to face Jax. "I just hope it works. But when we come back, we need to work on that pyramid paper."

Jax rolled his eyes. "You had to mention that, didn't you?"

JT took a deep breath. *I hope this is a good time.* She rang the doorbell.

Moments later, May, the youth pastor's wife, opened the door. "Oh, hi, JT. Is everything okay?"

JT looked down. "Not really. Do you guys have a few minutes?"

"Of course. Come on in and have a seat."

JT followed her into the living room. She sat in a chair across from the couch where May had joined Pastor Rich.

Rich set his book down. "Hi, JT. Congrats on the science fair last night. That floating bear was pretty sweet."

Caught off-guard, JT waved the compliment away. "Oh, thanks. But that's not why I stopped over."

"What's on your mind?"

JT had so much to tell them that she wasn't sure where to start. She stared at her hands, which were clutched in her lap. "Um…I need to talk to you about Jax and two of my other friends."

"Is something wrong with Jax?" Pastor Rich asked.

"Well…" She blushed. "He asked me out last night. I told him that I couldn't date him now because of his attitude toward God."

"I'm impressed," May said. "That must have been tough."

"It was." She glanced up at them shyly. "You guys know how I feel about him. And now I'm afraid that I just drove him farther away from God."

"You can't be responsible for someone else's faith—or lack of it," Rich said. "Of course, you have to be careful what you do and say around them, but ultimately, they are responsible for their own decision. You did the right thing by taking a stand for what God said is right." He paused before asking, "How did he take it?"

JT looked away. "Not very well. He got really upset and then started blaming God for his dad's death. I explained that it wasn't God's fault for all the bad stuff in this world, but he just told me that Genesis was nothing but a bunch of nice stories."

May leaned forward and clicked her tongue sympathetically. "Oh, honey, I'm so sorry. Is he still angry with you?"

Shaking her head, JT took a deep breath. "No. He started to calm down after a while and even said that he might come with me to youth group this week."

"Really? This week would be perfect for someone like him. We got so many questions from my Easter series last month that I decided to go through some of the evidences for the Resurrection."

May turned toward her husband. "By the way, I was thinking that you should contact the youth and let them know that this would be a great week to invite a friend."

JT sat up and smiled. "That would be perfect—not just for Jax, but for my two other friends that are coming too. They might not feel too out of place then."

"That's a great idea. I'll get the word out." Rich looked at JT. "So who are these two other friends?"

"Micky and Izzy. We had a little debate about the age of the earth, and they agreed to talk to you about it. Would you be able to meet with us for a little bit after youth group?"

"Of course, I'd love to."

"Thanks. They believe in evolution because they think every scientist believes it." She paused for a moment as a thought struck her. "Oh, do you still keep in touch with Jonas Ellis?"

Ellis was one of the top students to ever graduate from Silicon Valley Prep and he was a Bible-believing Christian. JT had met him once when Pastor Rich invited him to speak to the youth group a year earlier.

"Yeah, he's working on his doctorate in astrophysics at Berkeley State University right now."

"That's what I thought. Would you be able to give me his phone number? I have a question for him."

"I don't think he would mind, but let me ask him just to be sure. I know that he's very careful about sharing his beliefs because he doesn't want to be kicked out of the program there."

"They could do that?" JT asked.

Rich grinned. "Well, Berkeley's not really a Christian school now, is it? Actually, a lot of science programs would do that. Most of the state schools won't even accept your high school science classes if you used a textbook that favored creationism. They don't want anyone to question their own religious beliefs."

"By religious beliefs, you mean billions of years and evolution, right?"

"Exactly." Rich folded his hands in his lap. "How about we spend a little time praying for Jax and your friends right now?"

The time machine hovered about forty feet above the edge of the parking lot at the Silicon Valley branch of the United States Bureau of Clean Energy Development.

"Hey, there's my dad's car," Jax said as he pointed across the parking lot.

"Oh, Jax, I was thinking about it. We'd better not move the vehicle much while we're filming. Even though the camera's mounted, it wouldn't look like it was filmed from a hotel window."

"Good point. I already disabled the audio recording, too."

Jax looked at the computer monitor. *Nine o'clock. We should see something soon.* A few minutes later, a black car pulled up near the back entrance. He pointed at the vehicle. "Start recording."

"It doesn't have any license plates," Izzy whispered.

The car doors sprang open and three men dressed in black jumped out. As they headed for the door, Jax strained to hear them speaking, but he couldn't understand what they were saying. *Is that Spanish?* "Are you getting this?"

"Yeah. Just sit still."

When the first person reached the door, he pulled out a card and passed it over the scanner. The door opened, and the men quickly moved inside.

"I hope this will give the authorities enough information to lead them to these guys," Izzy said. "You sure we're far enough away? This thing is going to blow any minute."

"We're fine. There wasn't any debris this far out."

After several minutes, a large explosion ripped through the center of the building. A few seconds after the first blast, another explosion caused a fireball to shoot through the roof. Shockwaves rocked the car as a thick cloud of smoke filled their view.

Jax's stomach clenched. "My dad just died… and I sat here and did nothing."

Izzy put his hand on Jax's shoulder. "I'm really sorry, man, but we talked about this already. You know you couldn't have done—Hey, look."

Jax looked where Izzy was pointing. The smoke had cleared enough for him to notice the rear passenger door being pulled shut. As the car sped away, Jax said, "Quick! Let's follow them."

Izzy stopped recording. "You know we can't. We're just here to film the break-in."

Jax hesitated and then muttered, "Let's just go home."

THREE

"Hi, Jax."

Jax knelt at his locker searching for his computer science textbook. JT's voice sent a stab of ice through his gut. He had been dreading this moment all weekend. *Okay, here goes. Stay positive.* He looked at her and smiled. "Hey, what's up?"

"I was on my way to class, and I wanted to say 'hi' and to see how your mom was doing. You left so suddenly the other night, and I didn't see her at church yesterday."

While she was speaking, Jax pulled the last of his books out of his locker. "It's a long story. Maybe we could talk about it after school. He stood and closed the door. "I could walk you home." He turned slowly to gauge her reaction.

She smiled. "I'd like that."

I couldn't stay mad at her even if I wanted to. "Cool. Better run. Class is about to start. I'll see you second hour."

Mr. Li cleared his throat. "Congratulations to all of you that took part in the science fair over the weekend. "As expected, it was a great success."

The chatter in the room grew louder.

"Alright." Mr. Li raised his voice. "It's time to settle down. I know you're all catching that senioritis bug, but you're only sophomores and juniors, so I won't allow you guys to slack off for the next two weeks. We still have a lot to cover. Turn to chapter sixteen and we'll get started."

After finding the page, Jax leaned over slightly and whispered to Micky. "So did you pass?"

She reached into her purse on the floor and pulled out her wallet. Opening it up, she revealed her newly obtained driver's license.

Jax grinned. "And I thought you were the photogenic one."

"You're just jealous," Micky flipped her ponytail over her shoulder and stuck her nose in the air.

"Jax, Micky, that's enough," Mr. Li said. "In our last unit, we ended by discussing how the moon's gravity causes our ocean tides. For the rest of this week…"

Jax's mind wandered for the rest of the lecture, so he was surprised when Mr. Li finished early.

Jax, Izzy, JT, and Micky moved their desks together to take advantage of the few minutes of free time.

"So I saw on the news that the reporters dogged you." Izzy said.

"Yeah, they were jerks," Micky said. "They didn't believe anything we told them. And"—she raised her voice so everyone could hear her—"it's all because of Ted and William."

William turned in his chair. "Enough already.

Dude, we already apologized. What more do you want from us?"

"Give me a thousand bucks, and we'll call it even."

"Forget it."

Micky turned back to her group and they shared a laugh. "Man, those guys are fun to tease."

"At least they take it well," JT said.

"And they always walk right into it," Jax said, and they all laughed again.

"Oh, I almost forgot," JT said as she raised her hand. "Mr. Li, we were just wondering, would the dinosaurs have had the same constellations as us?"

Out of the corner of his eye, Jax saw the surprise on Micky's face.

"Talk about random," William said.

Mr. Li scratched his head for a moment. "No, I don't think they would have. The stars that are in our night sky—or maybe I should say, the stars that would be in our night sky if there weren't so many city lights around here—would have been in completely different locations relative to earth millions of years ago."

The bell rang the moment the last word left his mouth. As the students packed up their books to head out, JT nudged Micky with her elbow and said with a smile, "I guess I'll see you and Izzy at youth group on Wednesday."

"Don't remind me," she said with a huff.

35

"Oh, I better not forget this," Jax said to himself as he pulled a plastic bag containing a medium-sized sealed envelope out of his locker. He shut his locker and turned to see JT walking toward him. "Did you still want me to walk you home?"

"Yeah, are you ready?"

They started walking down the hallway to the exit. The 'floating bear' was still the talk of the school and several students made comments to JT about it.

"Wow, you and Micky must be the most popular kids in school right now," Jax said as they stepped out into a beautiful sunny afternoon.

She blushed a little. "Well, I can guarantee that you would be far more popular if you had entered your project."

Jax knew she was right and he felt a sense of pride in what he had done. "Speaking of 'the project,' Mr. Li was supposed to talk to you and Micky today about our trip. Did he?"

"Yep, he called us in during study hall."

"What did you tell him?"

"At first, we weren't sure if we should say anything. After all, it's pretty much top secret. But I also knew your grades were riding on it, and I didn't want Izzy to lose his 4.0."

He chuckled. "What? You weren't concerned about my GPA?"

She laughed too. "He assured us it would be

confidential, so we told him what happened."

"So, that was it?"

"Yeah, that's it. Why?"

"Did he say anything about my grade?"

"Oh, I didn't think you really cared about that," she said while thickly laying on the sarcasm. "I'm sure you guys will do fine, but I don't think he had talked to Izzy yet."

For a while they walked without speaking, then JT glanced sideways at him. "Um, I hope it's okay if I bring this up, but we never finished our conversation from the other night. Are you doing okay?"

His heart had been broken, but ironically, being near her made it better. "Yeah, I'm actually doing pretty good. I told you that no matter how things turned out, being your friend meant everything to me. At the time, I wasn't sure if that was true or not, but now I know it is."

She smiled, giving him one more reminder why he liked her so much. "That's awesome. I was really hoping that we could still hang out and be best friends. Last time we went through this sort—"

"Last time I was a jerk. I never should have ignored you like that. I guess I learned my lesson." He looked down and kicked a small rock down the road. "JT, I would still love to go out, but I can live with just being friends."

"Jax…Thank you."

37

They walked in silence for a few moments before she spoke again. "There's something else we need to talk about."

"Are you talking about God again?" Jax rolled his eyes and smiled.

"Yes. I know you're really mad at God because of what happened and it takes time to get over things like that." She stopped and grabbed his arm, turning him toward her. "And I know that it's okay to have questions about these sorts of things. I'd love to answer them for you or point you to someone else who can. I just really want you to know God the way that I do."

"Look, you know I don't believe all that stuff in the Bible." Jax held her gaze. "Even though we go to the same church, I've just never really bought into it. I'm glad that it makes you happy. I really am. But there are just too many problems, too many questions that can't be answered. Not to mention that we're at the top science school in the country, and we've learned a bunch of facts that contradict the Bible." He turned and continued walking.

She paused momentarily and then hustled to catch up. "Have you ever really tried to find answers to your questions?"

Have I ever tried...What kind of question is that? He closed his eyes and calmed himself. "What do you mean?"

"I mean," she said as she brushed her bangs away from her eyes, "have you ever really stopped and taken the time to see if there are legitimate answers?"

He thought for a few moments. "No, I guess not. I just assumed that there aren't any good answers since there's so much evidence against the Bible."

"Well, what if I could answer all of them for you?"

He nudged her with his elbow. "I thought you said that you don't have all the answers."

"I don't. But I know God does." Her green eyes sparkled. "How about we make a deal? You don't get mad at God anymore without first asking me about the problem that you're having?"

"You really want to listen to all of my problems and questions?" Jax was doubtful, yet hopeful, that she would be willing to devote that kind of time to him—even on something he had no intention of changing his mind about.

"Sure. If there's something I can do to help you see that God loves you, I'm willing to do it." She bit her bottom lip before speaking again. "There's one other…Hey, where are you going?"

Without warning, he had turned to his left. He held up the plastic bag. "I've got to drop this off in the mailbox near the bank. You wanna come with me?"

"Sure. What is it?"

"It's a secret."

"But…it's a secret that you're going to let me in on, right?" She batted her eyelashes.

Jax laughed and knew there was no way he was going to stay silent. All she had to do was flash her smile. "Yeah, of course."

"So what is it?"

"It's a memory card."

"A memory card? So what's on it?"

He grinned. "Well, that's the secret."

"Jax!" she raised her voice in mock frustration.

"Alright, alright. I'll tell you." He hesitated for a moment as he tried to decide where to start. "Remember the other night when my mom called?" She nodded. "Well, when I got home there were two government agents at my house. They had been talking to my mom for hours."

"About what?"

"They were re-opening the investigation surrounding my dad's death. And they said that he might have been in on some conspiracy gone wrong." He proceeded to tell her the rest of the story about that night. When he started telling her about the trip he and Izzy made, she interrupted him.

"You can't keep making trips in the time machine without me and Micky."

"Why not? It's my invention."

"Yeah, but you're using *our* technology without *our* permission."

He put his hands in his pockets and looked away. "I guess I didn't think you would mind."

She sped ahead, then turned around and walked backward while facing him. "Look, I'm excited that you have a chance to clear your dad's name and maybe give the authorities some more info about that night. But, you can't just keep making trips like that."

He held his hands up. "I can't believe you're getting mad about that."

"I'm not mad. I'm just … it's just that, it's too dangerous and I don't want anything to happen to you guys—not without me."

Her concern gave him hope…and made him curious. *Why does she care so much about everyone else?*

"Yeah, that's exactly what happened, Mr. Li," Izzy said. He had spent the past ten minutes explaining to his teacher how the time machine had actually worked.

Mr. Li leaned back in his chair and let out a long breath. "I checked with JT and Micky and they told similar stories. It's just so hard to believe you guys actually invented a time machine. Do you realize how important that would be?"

"Of course, and that's why it must be kept secret. Remember, you promised not to say anything."

"I know, I know. It's just going to be hard to keep something like that a secret. Besides, if you're telling the truth, you know you're going to have to take me on a trip sometime." Mr. Li smiled. "Actually, it's probably better if you don't use it anymore. You're lucky you didn't alter anything."

"Yeah, Jax and I talked about how we need to be really careful."

"Okay, Isaiah. I've seen all your calculations and the project itself. I'll take those into consideration. Have a good night."

"Thanks, Mr. Li. You too."

Izzy left the classroom and noticed that Micky was at her locker, which was close to his own. Several upper classmen had stopped by to congratulate her. "What are you still doing here?" Izzy said as he opened his own locker.

"I can't get away from all my fans," she said with a grin.

He quickly packed up his books for the night. Just as he finished, she walked over to him. "I can't believe we let JT talk us into going to youth group on Wednesday."

They walked down the hall toward the parking lot and Izzy noticed the walls looked bare without all the science fair posters. "Well, you gotta admit, she won that debate fair and square."

"Yeah, I know. I still think there's another explanation for it, though."

"I do, too. I don't know how anyone can really think that earth is only six thousand years old—especially someone as smart as JT."

"It's almost like she's been brainwashed by that church of hers."

Wow, that's just what I was thinking. "It sure seems like it. You know, Jax told me that she turned him down the other night. She said she couldn't date someone that didn't believe what she did."

"Really? Jax asked her out?"

"Yeah, he said she gave him some story about how she can't date him because he didn't love God."

Micky rolled her eyes. "I thought that's what she would say. We talked about it last week. Poor Jax."

"I just can't believe she could be so narrow-minded. Who cares whether or not someone believes in God? They would be perfect for each other."

"I know, right? It's too bad she doesn't see it. You know, I don't get her. She's so nice to everyone, but she's still so intolerant."

"I don't get her either. Then again, I don't understand girls in general."

Micky chuckled as she unlocked her car door. "Need a lift?"

"Um…I'd better not. Remember, I only take safe rides."

"Very funny. Get in."

"Okay, but you'd better get me home in one piece."

This is for you, Dad. Jax carefully lifted the opening of the bag to the mouth of the mail box. Once the open end of the bag was in, he lifted the bottom of the plastic bag, sending the package sliding down into the box. *Good, no fingerprints.*

When they started walking again, JT said, "Hey, I was thinking. Since you used our hover technology without our permission, you owe me a favor."

"Oh, really? Who says?"

"I do."

Jax chuckled. "Well, if *you* say so. What's the favor?"

"Since Micky and Izzy are coming to youth group on Wednesday night, then you should to come too."

"Doesn't look like I have a choice."

"Come on, be serious. You said you would look for answers."

"I know. I have been thinking about it, and I'll go."

She smiled and skipped a little. "Awesome."

Jax waved at his neighbor who drove past them.

They walked silently for a while before JT's face turned serious. "Can I bring up something else from Friday night?"

"Hey," he said as he stopped walking. "I'm really sorry that I got so mad the other night. I shouldn't have yelled at you."

"That's okay. We all get emotional and struggle with things. I won't hold it against you, alright?

"Thanks."

"But that's not what I wanted to talk about."

Uh-oh. Jax shifted his weight to one side. "Um…okay. What's up?"

She took a deep breath and then started walking. "Well, you asked me how an all-loving and all-powerful God could allow your dad to die. We never finished that part of the conversation."

Jax quietly breathed a sigh of relief. *Good. It's not about dating.* "Oh, there's more to it?"

"Yeah, lots more. But before I deal with that question, I'm gonna turn things around on you for a minute. Let's assume that there is no God, okay?"

He nodded.

"If there is no God to create everything, then either matter is eternal or everything had to come into existence by itself, right?"

"Sure, we've covered the big bang and evolution in several classes. They are proven facts."

"Hold on." She shook her head. "I'm not going

there, but I would strongly disagree with you that they are proven facts. We can talk about that later, but let's get back to what I was saying."

Jax fought the urge to defend his views and decided to hear her out. "Go ahead."

"Alright, if there is no God, then the world came into existence by itself. Sometime later, life evolved from nonliving materials, and millions or billions of years later, here we are, right?"

"That's pretty much what we've been taught all along."

She looked right at him. "I know, but it's wrong."

"How do you know it's wrong?"

"Because if it were true, we couldn't be having this discussion."

Jax held up his hands. "Whoa, slow down. You lost me. What does this discussion have to do with whether or not creation or evolution is true?"

"Well, if evolution were true, then our bodies are nothing more than the accidental combinations of random chemicals coming together at just the right time and place. If we are nothing but accidental random combinations, then how can you trust your own thinking?"

"Because I have a brain that follows the laws of logic."

JT laughed. "You do? Could have fooled me." As she said the words, she pushed him playfully on the shoulder. He was laughing too. "But where do those laws of logic come from? They aren't some sort of physical object that you can grab and examine. They're ideas, concepts, rules, and etcetera. They don't have a physical existence, and yet we know they do exist."

"I still don't see what you're getting at."

"Jax, if our brains are the results of accidents, then we have no reason to trust our own thinking. Not only that, the fact that we recognize laws of logic shows that we believe in things that are beyond this physical realm. The evolutionary viewpoint cannot hold to this position, because for them, everything is physical."

He let her words percolate in his mind for a minute before it hit him. *She's right.* "So let me get this straight. You're saying that if there is no God that created us, then it would be impossible to know whether or not you are thinking logically?"

"Pretty much. But there's more to it than that. If evolution is true, then it is impossible for a person to make any choices. They would have no will at all, because every decision would be determined for them by the chemical reactions in their brains."

"I've never even thought of that before, but it makes sense. So in other words, if the atheistic view of the world is right, then people think the way they do because of the chemicals in their brain."

"Right. You could say that I'm a Christian

because I have to be, and the atheist is an atheist because he has to be."

"Or," Jax jumped in, "a murderer is a murderer because he has to be." He paused to let that thought sink in and shuddered. *What a horrible way to view the world.* "Are there any atheists that recognize this?"

"There are some. I remember watching a video at youth group where an evolutionary professor was going on about how since evolution is true, we have no free will. He even said that there is no such thing as morality. It made me wonder why he tried so hard to convince people that Christianity is wrong."

"Well, maybe he could just say that he has to do it because of his chemical makeup."

"Or, maybe he's just being inconsistent."

Jax felt as though a dark cloud was lifting away from his mind. Somehow, he felt lighter and everything looked brighter. Suddenly, Friday night seemed like a distant memory. *Here I am with JT. We're not dating, but I'm still having a great time.*

"Can I get you a glass of lemonade and we can sit on the porch for a while?" she asked.

Startled from his mini-daydream, he looked up to see they had arrived at her house. "Um, I'd really like to, but I need to make sure my mom's doing okay."

"Oh." She seemed disappointed. "So far we've

only talked about how atheism doesn't make sense. I didn't really answer your question about God and suffering."

"That's alright. You gave me enough to think about for now. We can talk about that later."

She bounded up the porch steps. "Then I guess I'll see you at school tomorrow."

Four

Milk shot out of Micky's nose." "You did what?"

"Hey, keep it down." Izzy looked around the cafeteria and then leaned close. "Nobody can know about this stuff."

"It was something I had to do," Jax said.

Micky wiped her face with a napkin, took a deep breath and lowered her voice. "Look, you can't just take off with our stuff like that. I think it was a noble thing to do, but we should make an agreement that nobody uses the time machine for any reason unless all four of us agree on it." She glanced at JT. "Right?"

JT leaned back in her chair. "I agree."

"Yeah, but why should I agree to that?" Jax asked. "Izzy and I built it. We can use it whenever we want."

"Not with our repulsors on it," Micky said. "Besides, it's safer this way. We have to be very careful about using it. We could mess up everything by altering the past. So I think it would be best for us to plan our trips thoroughly before ever going back."

Jax grudgingly accepted that she was right. He didn't like it, but he knew he couldn't argue. "Alright, I agree. No one uses the machine unless all of us agree…except in emergency situations like when Izzy was in the tree."

"Good point. How 'bout you, Izzy?"

"Yeah, sure, I'm in."

"Well now that that's settled," JT said, looking at Micky, "are you still planning on going to youth group tonight?"

"Girl, you just aren't gonna leave that alone, are you?"

"Not a chance," JT said.

"Yeah, I'll be there. I can even pick you up now that I got my license."

"Cool. Be at my place by 6:15 since it starts at 6:30." She turned to Jax and Izzy. "How about you guys?"

"Sure, JT. You even got Mr. Li to admit you were right," Izzy said. "I'll be there if I can get a ride with a safe driver," he said as he winked at Micky.

"Hey, I got you home the other day," Micky said.

"Yeah, barely."

"Don't worry, Iz," Jax said. "I'll pick you up."

"I thought I said a safe driver."

They all laughed.

Micky wiped her sweaty hands on her pants as the foursome entered Mountain View Bible Church. "This will be the first time I've ever been in a church."

"Are you serious?" Izzy asked.

"Well, my mom was raised as a Hindu in India, and my dad is an atheist."

"I figured pretty much everyone has been to church before," Izzy said. "I used to go a lot when I was younger, but then my parents stopped going when they got divorced, so I did too."

"I'm guessing this will be way different than what you guys expect. In fact, I think you'll really like it," JT said. She led the group through the foyer and then up the stairs to the large youth room.

Micky looked all around her. *Wow, JT was right. This place is sweet.*

The middle of the room contained nearly fifty soft, comfortable chairs facing a small stage. The outlying areas of the room were filled with several couches, a row of computers, a ping-pong table, pool table, and foosball table. Several teenagers were milling around in each area.

"JT!"

Micky noticed an average-height girl with shoulder-length dark brown hair running toward them.

"Emma." JT greeted her friend with a hug. "This is Micky, Jax, and Izzy."

Micky shook Emma's hand. "Nice to meet you."

"You too," Emma said. She looked at JT. "I've gotta get back to my game. I'll talk to you later."

When she had gone, JT led her friends over to Pastor Rich, calling out hellos and responding to greetings along the way.

"Hey guys. Welcome," Pastor Rich said as he shook their hands and smiled. "Jax, it's good to see you." He glanced at his watch. "Hey, maybe we can catch up after? It's time to get things started."

Jax nodded, and Micky thought he looked relieved.

They found seats as Pastor Rich stepped onto the stage. He began with some brief announcements and a prayer, and when he finished, several students, including JT, walked up to the stage to lead the group in singing.

Jax, Izzy, and Micky stood along with the rest of the group when the music started. To her surprise, Micky found herself swaying to the rhythm. *I always thought that church would be boring. The band rocks—and that drummer sure is cute.*

Micky didn't sing. She looked at Izzy and noticed he wasn't singing either. Jax looked nervous, but his mouth was moving. She grinned. *He would do anything for that girl.*

"Thank you praise band," Pastor Rich said after he bounded up to the stage and grabbed a mic.

Jax watched as JT and the other musicians returned to their seats.

Micky leaned over. "JT, you totally rock, girl. How come you didn't tell me you were in a band?"

JT smiled. "You never asked."

Pastor Rich opened his Bible and placed it on a small podium. "Tonight is an exciting night. I have the privilege of sharing with you about the most important event in history.

"Last month we celebrated Easter, which is when we focus on Jesus rising from the dead. At the time, I talked a little bit about the importance of the Resurrection, and how it relates to our salvation, but I didn't spend too much time talking about the amazing amount of evidence we have for it.

"Since then, many of you have been asking me questions on how we can have confidence that Jesus really did rise from the dead. Those are what I want to focus on tonight, but feel free to ask questions along the way."

Jax glanced at JT. She sat quietly and held a notebook on her lap, with her Bible underneath that, and a pen in her hand. In the past, whenever his mom had made him go to youth group, Jax had tuned out the message. But tonight he felt he owed it to JT to pay attention.

Rich walked to the other side of the stage. "For the past two thousand years, many people have tried desperately to explain away the Resurrection, only to fail again and again. They have tried just about every idea you can think of, yet one thing becomes clearer with every attempt to explain it away: Jesus died on the cross, was laid in a tomb, and rose from the dead three days later."

"How can you be sure that He actually died on the cross?" an unfamiliar voice asked.

Jax turned and spotted a tall, shaggy-haired guy wearing a T-shirt from a local high school.

"For that matter, how can you even be sure that He ever lived?"

Jax looked back at the pastor to see how he would handle that challenge.

Pastor Rich pointed at the boy, and his eyes lit with excitement. "Those are good questions. Let me answer your second question first. The idea that Jesus never really existed is rejected by almost every scholar today—both Christian and unbeliever. The reason is that there is so much evidence to show that He was a real person. Not only do we have four eyewitness accounts in the Bible: Matthew, Mark, Luke, and John, we also have the writings of several non-Christian authors from the same time period. In other words, even those who weren't Christians wrote about Him."

He pushed up the sleeves of his sweater. "Your other question has been the subject of a couple of theories surrounding the Resurrection. There's a view out there called the Swoon Theory, which says that Jesus didn't really die on the cross, but just fell into a coma-like state. After being put in the tomb, He revived, escaped, and acted like He rose from the dead."

"Yeah, that's what I was getting at," said the shaggy-haired guy.

"Well, you guys all have Bibles in the racks underneath your chairs. Grab one and turn to John 19:33…it's on page 953."

Jax retrieved a Bible. He placed it on his lap and stared at the cover. *Why should I read this? What's God ever done for me?*

JT leaned close to him and whispered. "Jax." She smiled as she held her open Bible closer to him. "You can look on with me."

Pastor Rich picked up his Bible. "This is the Crucifixion account written by John, who was one of Jesus' closest followers. He was the only disciple who was actually at the Crucifixion—the rest of them were in hiding. Look what John wrote here:

"'But when they came to Jesus and found that He was already dead, they did not break His legs. Instead, one of the soldiers pierced Jesus' side with a spear, bringing a sudden flow of blood and water.'"

Passion infused Pastor Rich's voice as he read on. "Now look at what's next. It's interesting because it seems like John doesn't know why blood and water flowed from the wound, but he knows it did because he saw it.

"He wrote, 'The man who saw it has given testimony, and his testimony is true. He knows that he tells the truth, and he testifies so that you also may believe.'"

Rich set the Bible down and started pacing again. "So even though John probably had no idea why he saw blood and water, several medical experts have shown that this is what we would expect to happen to someone who was tortured the way Jesus was. He was flogged, beaten, had a crown of thorns pushed onto His head, and, of course, crucified. If a person goes through that sort of beating, he begins to experience a condition called hypovolemic shock. This causes the heartbeat to increase and leads to the buildup of a clear fluid around the lungs and heart. Apparently, these buildups were punctured by the spear that pierced Him, which is why John saw what looked like blood and water flowing out of Jesus' side. That means that Jesus actually did die on the cross."

He actually used science to back up his beliefs. Jax looked at his friends. JT was taking notes and Izzy seemed to be paying attention. *JT said he had answers. Maybe she's right.* He did a double-take when he saw Micky raise her hand.

"You've been making a strong case for what you believe, but you keep on using the Bible. How do you know that you can trust what's in there? Don't you think the writers had an agenda to push?"

"Those are excellent questions." Rich held out

a hand in her direction. "You're right. They did have an agenda to push. We all have presuppositions, beliefs we bring to the table whenever we examine a set of evidence. For me, I believe the Bible is the Word of God and is one hundred percent accurate, so it's natural for me to start there.

"I could stand here and use only the facts that are accepted by nearly everyone, even the scholars that don't believe in the Resurrection. They still accept that Jesus died, the tomb was empty, and that His followers started preaching about the Resurrection from the earliest days of the church. The interesting thing is that with just this evidence, Jesus rising from the dead still makes the most sense.

"But let me answer your question about whether or not we can trust the Bible. First, just because someone might have an agenda, doesn't mean that he is wrong. For example, when you do your math homework, you have an agenda to get a good grade. So you write that two plus two equals four. Even though you had an agenda, this is still true. You can question the motives of the people who wrote the Bible, but you still have to see if what they said is true or false.

"The Bible is a unique book. It was written over a fifteen hundred year time period by more than forty different authors without any contradictions. But the biggest thing that makes the Bible different from the holy books of other religions is that it has hundreds of detailed prophecies that have been fulfilled to the letter. No other holy book has anything like that. Let me give you a few examples, and then we'll get back to the Resurrection.

"In Isaiah, which was written more than 700 years before Jesus was born, God predicted that the Jews would be captured and taken away to another country called Babylon." Rich leafed through the Bible on the podium. "In chapters 44 and 45, God told the Jews that they would be sent back to their homeland and be allowed to rebuild their city, Jerusalem. He said that the man who would allow them to do this would be named Cyrus. At the time this was written, the Jews were still in their homeland.

"History tells us that Babylon did capture the Jews. After that Babylon was defeated by the Persian Empire. Later, a king named Cyrus told the Jews they could go back to their land and rebuild Jerusalem. Keep in mind that God named this guy about 150 years before he was ever born. And God told us exactly what this man would do."

Jax stared at a pattern in the carpet. *Now he's using history.*

Pastor Rich spoke louder and moved toward the students. "In Isaiah 53, we are told that Jesus would come, die for people's sins, and then rise from the dead. Daniel, who lived over five hundred years before Christ, predicted the exact time when Jesus would be killed.

"In Psalm 22, the writer provides a graphic description of Jesus' crucifixion, one thousand years before it happened—three hundred years before crucifixion was even invented.

"These are just a handful of hundreds of precise prophecies that have been fulfilled. No other holy book comes close, because only God can tell the future, and He is the One that inspired the Bible.

"So when the Bible says that Jesus died and rose again, I believe it." He looked at Micky. "Does that help answer your questions?"

Micky nodded and sank back in her chair.

Jax thought deeply about what he was hearing as Pastor Rich continued talking about some of the proofs for the Resurrection. *I've heard about the empty tomb, but over five hundred people saw Him alive again. That's incredible.*

Pastor Rich paused and slowly scanned the group of students. "Finally, let me make sure you understand why Jesus did all of these things. The Bible tells us that we are all sinners. We have all rebelled against God. If you don't believe that, just compare your own life to some of God's laws. Have you ever told a lie?" He raised his hand. "Have you ever been disobedient to your parents?" Again he raised his hand. "We all have, so we're all guilty. We deserve the punishment for breaking God's rules. And the Bible tells us that our punishment is death and judgment. Because we are sinful, we deserve God's wrath.

"Some people will tell you that God doesn't punish sin, but He does. He has to do it, because He is perfectly just. And a just judge has to punish those that break the law. Think about it. How would you feel if somebody robbed you and then the judge let him off the hook? If he was a good judge, he would make sure that the thief paid for his crime. Since God is the perfect Judge, why should we think He will let us off the hook?

"But that's where Jesus comes in. John 3:16 states, 'For God so loved the world that He gave His only begotten Son, that whoever believes in Him should not perish but have everlasting life.'

"You see, Jesus is God, and He was willing to become a man, so that He could take our place. When He was on the cross, He took on the punishment for the sins of the whole world, so that we wouldn't have to pay the infinite penalty of our sin…so that we wouldn't have to spend eternity in the lake of fire. That's the good news. Even though we deserve judgment, we don't have to suffer for eternity.

"Romans 10:9 says, 'That if you confess with your mouth the Lord Jesus and believe in your heart that God has raised Him from the dead, you will be saved.' That's it. There's nothing you can do to earn it. Salvation is only available by God's grace alone, and it is received by faith alone in Jesus Christ alone.

"Remember, not only did He predict that He was going to die, but He also said that He would rise again three days later. He proved it by appearing to His disciples and then to over five hundred people at once. If you reject His offer of salvation, you will have no excuse when you stand before God. Let's pray."

After the prayer, Pastor Rich headed for the back of the room as the praise band took the stage for the final song.

During the singing, Jax strode over to the pastor. "Can I talk to you for a few minutes?"

FIVE

"Have a seat," Pastor Rich said, closing his office door behind him.

Jax looked around the room and saw a large wooden desk to his left with floor-to-ceiling bookcases lining the wall behind it. He sat down at a small table with four chairs near the middle of the room.

"So, what did you need to talk to me about?" Rich asked as he grabbed a chair to Jax's left.

Jax gathered his thoughts before speaking. "Well, I've been doing a lot of thinking lately. JT has been answering some of my questions, but it seems like each time she gives me an answer, I think of two more questions. But tonight, everything you said…every word, made sense. Deep down, I know that what you were saying is right. Jesus really did die in my place on the cross and He really did rise again."

He leaned over and buried his head in his hands. "But I just have so many questions. I don't understand why God would let my dad die. I don't believe God would ever send someone to hell. I don't believe there was ever a worldwide flood and I don't believe that JT is right about the age of the earth. I mean, there's no way that—"

Rich held up a hand. "Whoa, slow down a little. We can talk about all those things if you want, but right now there's something else you need to do."

Jax looked up. "What do you mean?"

"Jax, you need to get things straight with God before you worry about anything else." His green eyes locked onto Jax's. "Those other issues are extremely important, but you may not ever find the answers you're looking for unless you have Christ in your life."

"Why?"

"You know the saying, 'seeing is believing,' right?"

"Yeah."

Rich took a deep breath. "Well, in many cases, it's not true. It's really 'believing is seeing.' Look, the reason that you don't accept a young earth, a worldwide flood, and whatever other areas you question is not due to a lack of evidence. It's because you already believe the other view is right. Therefore, when you look at this world, you think of it in terms of an evolutionary origin. What you already believe oftentimes determines what you allow yourself to see. Does that make sense?"

Jax shrugged. "I'm not sure."

"Okay, let me give you a football analogy. Let's say the quarterback of the team you're cheering for throws a pass to a receiver in the end zone. It looks like it's going to be a touchdown, but just before the ball gets there, the defender trips the receiver and the pass falls incomplete. You would probably be yelling for a pass interference penalty, but the other team's fans would say it was just incidental contact. However, if we reverse the situation, then you would be claiming it was incidental contact and the other fans would be yelling for a penalty. Your bias for your team affects how you see the game. Does that make sense?"

"Yeah, I see what you're saying."

"We could be here all night talking about your questions, and I would be happy to address them. But you need to get right with God first. You mentioned that you don't believe God would send somebody to hell, right?"

"Yeah, I mean, it doesn't make any sense that God would send a good person there."

Rich leaned back in his chair and rubbed his chin for a few seconds. "What would you say if I told you I agreed with you?"

Jax's eyes widened. "You mean you don't believe that people go to hell?"

"That's not what I said. I said I agreed with you that God would not send a *good* person to hell."

Jax furrowed his brow and scratched his cheek. "I don't know what you mean."

"Let me ask you some questions and then we'll come back to your statement, okay?"

Jax nodded once, still unsure of where this conversation was headed.

"Have you ever told a lie?"

Taken aback by the question, he smirked. "Of course. Who hasn't?"

"Okay, so what does that make you?"

The smirk quickly left his face as he thought about his response. "I guess it makes me a liar."

Rich nodded. "Have you ever stolen anything? It doesn't matter how valuable it was."

Jax thought for a few moments and then said, "Yeah, I remember taking some change out of my mom's purse one time."

"And what does that make you?"

He hesitated. "A thief."

"Just one more question. The Bible says you shall not commit adultery. Jesus said that if you look at a girl with lust then you have already committed adultery with her in your heart. Have you ever lusted after a girl?"

Jax knew he was guilty again and nodded.

"Those three questions were based on the Ten Commandments, some of the standards God set for His people to follow. We may not be under the same Law the Israelites were, but God's principles don't change. That was only three of them. Would you like to go through all the rest?"

Jax shook his head, realizing he wouldn't like the outcome.

"Okay, so you just admitted to me that you were a liar, a thief, and an adulterer at heart. So when you stand before God and He judges you according to His standard, do you think you will be found innocent or guilty?"

"I, um." Instinctively Jax wanted to proclaim his innocence, but he had a strong conviction that told him otherwise. "I would be guilty."

"So would God let you into heaven, or would He send you to the lake of fire?"

Once again, his gut reaction was to defend himself, but he knew the truth. "I guess I would go to the lake of fire, right?"

Rich looked Jax straight in the eyes and nodded slowly. "You see there really is no such thing as a 'good' person when they are compared to God's standard. That's why I said that He wouldn't send any good people there. There aren't any. We have all broken His law, and we all deserve His punishment. But Jesus came to bear our punishment, and He has promised to save all those who call on Him."

"Pastor Rich," Jax said as tears formed in his eyes. "I need Jesus."

Rich slid his chair closer to Jax and placed a hand on his shoulder. "There's no magic formula to this. Some people want to be led in prayer, and others just want to pour out their heart to God. I'll leave it up to you. Do you want to pray or do you want to repeat after me?"

"Um, I think I'll do it." Jax bowed his head and

closed his eyes. After a few moments of silence, interrupted only by his sniffles, he prayed. "Dear God, I know that I've done a lot of bad things ... I've broken Your commands and I know I deserve hell ... God, I also believe that You sent Jesus to the earth to take my place on the cross, to take my punishment. I don't know everything that I need to do, but I know that I need You. I believe that You raised Jesus from the dead and promised eternal life to all who trust in You. I need You ... I need You to save me. I don't deserve Your love, but please, save me...Amen."

After talking to some of the other students for nearly ten minutes, JT finally had an opportunity to speak with just Micky and Izzy. "So what did you guys think?"

Micky glanced around at the small groups of teens hanging out, playing foosball or just talking. When her eyes fell on May, who was praying with a young lady that had come to youth group for the first time, they narrowed the tiniest fraction. Disappointment tugged at JT's heart.

"It was different," Micky said. "Very different than I expected."

"Is that a good different or a bad different?"

Micky smiled. "Oh, it was fine, especially that drummer. You have to set me up."

JT shook her head and half-smiled. "You're hopeless." She looked at Izzy. "So, what'd you think?"

"It was pretty cool, but we really need to get going. My mom's gonna flip if I'm out past 9:30 on a school night, especially since I was out late all last week."

"Okay," JT said. "Micky, it doesn't look like Jax is ready to leave. Do you mind taking Izzy home? I can find another ride."

"With Jax?" Micky teased.

"I don't know." She blushed slightly. "There are several people here to choose from." Inside she knew Micky was right. "Micky, please?"

"Sure, no problem. Come on, Iz."

"See you guys at school. Only seven days left."

"Yeah, seven days left and then summer classes," Izzy said.

"Ugh." JT shuddered.

"Later, girl."

"Bye." JT turned and looked toward the office. *What is taking them so long?* She waited around anxiously for a few minutes until she couldn't stand it any longer. *I have to know.* She walked to the door and tapped lightly on the glass.

Pastor Rich and Jax looked up. They had obviously been in a deep conversation. Her pastor looked at Jax, said a few words, and Jax nodded. Rich turned and motioned for her to enter.

71

"Sorry for interrupting." She sat down in an open chair. "Are you sure it's okay for me to be in here?"

"Sure. In fact, I'm glad you're here. Jax has something he wants to tell you," he said with a smile.

She looked at Jax and noticed his eyes were red. *Could it be true? Does he believe?*

He looked her in the eyes, smiled, and said, "JT, I've been in here talking with Pastor Rich about what he said tonight." He paused.

"And?"

"And, I wanted you to know…I wanted to tell you that I've asked Jesus to save me."

JT let the words sink in. When they did, she shrieked and lunged out of her chair, squeezing Jax around the neck as hard as she could. Tears of joy streaked down her face. *Thank You, Jesus! Thank You for saving Jax!* She held her constrictor-like grip until she heard, "JT, I can't breathe." She let go, stood up, and started pacing. "I…I'm so excited, I don't know what to say…I can't even sit down. Jax, I'm so happy for you."

"JT, thank you…for everything," Jax said. "Thank you for always being there for me, for your prayers, and for inviting me here tonight."

Tears still streamed down her face, and she stood speechless.

"Pastor Rich, thank you, too. I still don't know

if I believe everything in the Bible, but I know I can't deny what Jesus did for me."

"Feel free to stop in and talk to me at any time. There are good answers to your questions, and if I don't know the answer, then I'll find it for you."

"Thanks again," Jax said as he stood. Pastor Rich stood, too, and gave Jax a firm handshake.

"Welcome to the family—God's family." He turned toward JT. "Are you gonna make it?"

"Yeah, I'm just so happy right now." She gave Jax another hug and then gave one to Pastor Rich. "Oh, I almost forgot, I need a ride home. Micky and Izzy left."

Rich took a step forward. "No problem. May and I will give you a lift."

JT glanced at Jax, then nodded. "Thanks."

The three left the office and walked toward May, who was now alone on the couch.

"JT, can I talk to you for a moment?" Rich asked. "Jax, can you give us a minute?"

Jax nodded and kept walking.

Once Jax was out of earshot, the pastor said, "Be careful."

JT quirked an eyebrow. "What do you mean?"

"Look, I know how you feel about him, and how he feels about you, but a relationship isn't what he needs right now. He needs time to grow in the Lord, figure out who he is in Jesus. Does that make sense?"

Her gaze flicked from Rich to Jax and back again, then she nodded. "I understand."

He looked relieved. "Oh, one more thing. It's not a good idea for Jax to give you a ride home tonight."

Puzzled, JT asked, "Why not?"

"I'm not saying I don't trust you, but it's not a good idea for a guy and girl to be alone—especially when they already have feelings for each other. There are just too many temptations. And it can give rise to rumors which can damage your testimony—even if nothing happened."

"Oh, I never really thought about what other people might think. I'll be careful."

Jax arrived home that night feeling like a new man. *I am a new man. My sins are forgiven.* His mom was still in the living room when he walked into the house.

As he told her everything that happened that night, tears welled up in her eyes. She jumped off the couch and hugged him tightly. *And I thought JT had a strong hug.*

SIX

"Are you going to tell us where we're going?" Izzy asked.

"No way. It's a surprise," JT said. "As long as Jax follows my directions, we'll be there in about an hour."

"Can you give us a hint?" Micky asked.

"Sure." JT flashed a playful smile. "I promise you'll enjoy it and it will be educational. Plus, lunch is on me."

"It'd better be good—dragging me out this early on a Saturday morning," Micky said. "Not even Izzy can do anything with his hair at this hour."

Izzy laughed. "Hey, watch it."

Ten minutes after leaving Mountain View, Jax turned right onto Highway 84 to cross the Dumbarton Bridge.

"Hey, we need to take another trip," Micky said.

"We are taking a trip." Jax rolled his eyes.

Micky lightly slapped the back of Jax's head. "No, you dork. I mean we need to go back in time again. We're all here, so we can agree upon a place and time."

"That sounds like fun," JT said. "You got any ideas?"

"How about back to ancient India? I could see how my ancestors lived."

"I don't think so, Micky," Izzy said. "We'd

better do our best to stay away from civilization. We don't want to mess with anything in the past that might change our present world."

"Weren't you afraid of doing that the first time?" Micky asked.

"Yeah, we talked about it, but our curiosity got the best of us. Besides, we weren't even sure it was going to work. Of course now, with your hover technology, we can be pretty careful about not interacting with anything to a significant degree."

"Good point. So what if we just hovered around ancient India? If anybody saw us, they would just think the time machine was a UFO."

"Micky, you seriously need help," JT said as she nudged her. "I think I have a better idea."

Izzy twisted in his seat to face the girls. "Anything is better than Micky's idea. What is it?"

"What if we went back to the same place and time—"

"No way." Izzy held up his hand. "You aren't taking me back to that place."

"I thought any place would be better than my idea," Micky said. "How's India sound now?"

"Izzy, just listen for a minute," JT said. "I don't blame you for wanting to avoid it, but I think you should hear me out. What if we went back there, sort of like a controlled experiment. We could keep exploring the area to see what it's really like, and you could map it out."

"I'm listening."

"Plus, I think we should try to figure out once and for all who was right," JT said.

"Right about what?" Izzy asked.

"About the whole age of the earth issue. We have an opportunity to solve one of the greatest controversies of our time. We should come up with some detailed predictions of what we would expect to see if we were truly seventy million years in the past, or just forty-five hundred years. Once we're there, we could compare our predictions with what we find."

Izzy hesitated. "I'll do it on one condition."

"Name it."

"That when we are proven right, you'll stop bugging us about the Bible and the age of the earth."

Jax looked at her in the rearview mirror and could tell she was thinking it through. Finally, she spoke. "What about you Micky? Are you willing to agree that?"

"Sure. I just hope you aren't too disappointed when you see how wrong you are."

"Okay, so here's the deal. Oh wait, Jax, you'll need to go north here on 880." She turned back to Micky. "So, if my predictions based on the Bible are shown to be accurate, then you guys will admit that the whole evolutionary view is wrong, and you'll at least consider listening to what the

Bible says. But, if your list is shown to be true, then I'll stop talking about the Bible around you. Does that sound right?"

"What if it's a tie?" Jax asked.

"How can it be a tie?" Micky asked.

"Well, what if there are a couple of predictions from both lists that match what we see? We need to make sure that our lists are distinct enough to know which view is truly supported by the evidence."

"That should be easy enough," Izzy said. "So, JT, you wanna make that deal?"

"Yep, I'm in."

"Alright, me too," Micky said. "Jax?"

"I'm not big on going back there." He was thinking of their safety again—especially JT's—but he didn't want to say it.

"Why not?" Micky asked. "Is little Jaxy afraid?"

"Duh. I was almost an allosaurus appetizer. I've had enough danger for one lifetime."

"We'll be fine," Micky said. "Besides, we can just hover around and find a safe place to land. We'll stay as far away from those dinosaurs as possible. So, are you in?"

He still wasn't convinced that it was the wisest plan, but he didn't want to disappoint JT, and he had too many questions to miss an opportunity like this. "I guess so."

"Okay, so when do we want to do this?" Izzy asked.

After a brief silence, Micky said, "We should probably wait until school gets out. How about next Saturday? That way we would have the entire day to explore. Are you guys free?"

Forty minutes later, Jax pulled the car into a visitor's parking spot on the Berkeley State University campus. "What are we doing here?"

"You'll see," JT said. "I've got a surprise lined up for all of you."

They were walking through a large courtyard surrounded by dormitories when JT's phone rang. "Hello…Um, yeah. We just got here. In fact, I can see the building right now. We'll be there in just a minute. Are you already there? …Okay, we'll meet you inside."

"Who was that?" Micky asked.

"Your surprise."

The group continued walking toward a gigantic brick building directly in front of them. They soon stood in front of the School of Physical Sciences building.

"Wow, this place is huge," Izzy said.

"Are you guys coming?" JT asked as she started up the stairs. They followed her through the front doors and into the expansive lobby. She stopped and looked around.

"What are we looking for?" Jax asked.

JT said nothing for a moment as she scanned the room. "Found it. Let's go." She led the group down a long hallway to their left, past several lecture halls, and into a lobby.

A thin, dark-haired man in his mid-to-late twenties approached. "JT?"

"Mr. Ellis?"

"Yeah, it's good to see you guys. Welcome."

"Mr. Ellis, this is Micky, Jax, and Izzy," JT said as she pointed to each of them in turn. "Guys, this is Mr. Jonas Ellis."

"Nice to meet you Micky, Jax, Izzy," he said. "But, please, call me Jonas."

Jax thought JT stifled a giggle as the three of them stood speechless a moment. Forcing his tongue to work, he said, "You…You're *the* Jonas Ellis?"

Jonas pointed both hands toward himself and smiled. "In the flesh. It's great to see a bunch of young students from my alma mater. I've been so busy up here for the past nine years that I rarely make it back to the area. I know, that's pretty sad, since it's only an hour away."

Everyone at Silicon Valley Prep knew the name Jonas Ellis. He was a legend. He led the school to four consecutive state titles and two national titles in math and science competitions. He was named the National High School Science Student of the Year for both his junior and senior years. He was also the only SVP student to ever win the school's science fair twice.

Jonas clapped his hands once. "So should we go see what you came here for?"

"Yeah, let's do it," JT said.

Jonas led the four youth through a door into the Galileo Planetarium. As they walked in, he instructed them to have a seat somewhere near the middle of one of the back rows. "JT told me that I would be able to help clear up a little debate you guys were having. She said that you guys wanted to know where the stars would have been in relation to earth forty-five hundred years ago, and where they would have been seventy million years ago."

He started to walk to the back of the room, then paused and said, "Oh, if you guys have any questions, feel free to ask me afterward. I've only got permission to use this room for the next twenty minutes."

As the lights dimmed, Jax leaned to his right and asked, "JT, how do you know Jonas Ellis?"

"I was just going to ask that," Micky said.

JT grinned and said, "I'll tell you after the show."

The room grew completely dark before the domed ceiling lit up with dots of light representing thousands of stars. Jonas spoke from behind them as he operated the computer controlling the projector. "This is what our night sky looks like on a summer evening. Let me highlight some of the constellations for you. Here is Ursa Major, which contains the Big Dipper. Here's Ursa Minor with the Little Dipper. Here's Draco, the dragon. This W-shaped one is Cassiopeia. And here are the rest of them." As he said the last sentence, the rest of the dome lit up with dozens of constellations.

"Alright, JT, on the phone you mentioned the Big Dipper and Cassiopeia. I'm going to leave those two highlighted, but the rest will go back to normal. Now, let me show you what the sky would have looked like forty-five hundred years ago. We'll go back one thousand years per second here." There was a slight movement in the lights, but it was hardly noticeable. "As you can see, at forty-five hundred years, the night sky is almost identical. The stars have only shifted slightly. You can still make out the Big Dipper and Cassiopeia. Here are the rest of them." Once again, the dome was brightened by the highlighted constellations.

"Okay, let me take those down again. We'll just keep our original two constellations highlighted. Now, let's go back seventy million years. To do this, we'll have to go faster than a thousand years per second. That would take over nineteen hours. So we're going to speed this up to half a million years per second. This will take just under two-and-a-half minutes."

The lights on the dome swirled in all directions. Within the first few seconds, JT could no longer identify any of the constellations. The lines connecting the lights for the Big Dipper and Cassiopeia were darted in every direction. The scene above them looked more like a laser light show than the night sky.

After the program ran its course, Jonas said, "As you can see, the constellations would have been unrecognizable seventy million years ago. Although, you could make some new ones if you wanted," he chuckled as he highlighted a series of stars that formed an awkwardly shaped smiley face. "This could be the 'Have a Nice Day' constellation."

The teenagers laughed at his corny sense of humor and the lights soon came back on. "There's another group coming in here in a few minutes, so let's go to my office and we'll talk."

"So there's really no way that the stars could have been in the same position seventy million years ago, is there?" Micky asked as Jonas handed her a folded chair.

Jonas stepped around a telescope and sat behind his desk. "No, there's no way that they would have been even close to the same positions."

JT smiled. *I sure hope he can get through to her.*

"So how do you guys know each other?" Jax asked.

"Mr. Ellis spoke to our youth group last year about how science confirms what the Bible teaches," she said.

"Wait a minute. You believe the Bible too?" Izzy asked. "I thought you were one of the top science students in the country. How can you believe what the Bible claims?"

Jonas smiled and leaned forward. "I do believe what the Bible teaches—every word of it. My belief in the Bible doesn't hinder me from doing real science."

"But you're an astronomy major," Izzy said. "Everyone knows there are stars that are billions of light years away."

"Look, guys, there are a couple of really important things we need to discuss. First, I don't typically talk about my beliefs around here. I'm trusting you guys because I trust JT. I trust JT because Pastor Rich told me that I could."

"Are you saying that you're afraid to tell people that you're a Christian?" Jax asked.

"No, no, not at all. I mean, sure there are times that I'm a little nervous to bring it up around some people, but for the most part, I'm open about my belief in Christ."

"But I thought you just said that you don't talk about your beliefs around here."

"Right. What I meant was that I don't talk about the fact that I believe the earth is just thousands of years old."

"Why not?"

"Well, Jax"—Jonas leaned back in his chair and folded his hands behind his head—"I guess it's because I don't want to be thrown out of school."

"They wouldn't do that, would they?" Izzy asked.

"I'm pretty sure they would. You see, most of the professors and the administration around here don't really care if you're a Christian. They just do not accept biblical creationists."

"Well, that's because a person who believes that is obviously rejecting a ton of scientific evidence," Micky said.

"No, that's not it at all. We all have the same evidence. We—"

"No, we don't." Micky pointed to a poster of the night sky. "Creationists reject all the evidence that proves the earth is billions of years old."

"Actually, we do have the exact same evidence." He pointed to the same poster. "We look at the same stars and the same planets. We see the same rocks and trees. We even examine the same fossils. But we interpret that evidence differently because we have different worldviews."

"What do you mean by 'worldview'?" Izzy asked.

"Basically, it's how a person views the world. We all have starting points, or presuppositions— things we assume to be true—that we use to make sense of the things around us."

Jonas pointed to Izzy's glasses. "Think of it like a pair of glasses. If you put on glasses with red-colored lenses, then everything will look red to you. But if I put on blue ones, then everything I see will be blue. We could look at the same object and argue all day whether it is red or blue. If you assume evolution is true, then you will try to explain everything through that lens, just like I explain things through the lens of the Bible— that's my starting point."

"Okay, but the facts don't change no matter what you believe," Izzy said as he shrugged his shoulders.

"That's true. Let me give you an example." Jonas' eyes sparkled with excitement. "We all know the Grand Canyon exists. If I went there with one of my evolutionary classmates, we could both examine the canyon and reach vastly different conclusions. I could think that it took a lot of water over a short period of time to carve out the canyon, while my friend might think that it took a little bit of water over a long period of time."

Jonas sat up straight and scooted forward. "The Grand Canyon is the fact, but we have interpreted that fact differently because of our worldviews. It's important not to confuse your interpretation of the fact with the fact itself."

"Okay, but what about the starlight issue that Izzy mentioned?" Micky asked. "There's no way around that. The speed of light is constant, so those stars have to be billions of light years away."

"Well, first of all, remember that a light year is not a measure of time; it's a measure of distance equal to nearly six trillion miles. Don't be fooled by the name."

Jonas rested his hands on his desk. "I agree with you that there are stars that are billions of light years away, but that doesn't mean that it took billions of years for their light to reach Earth."

"But if the speed of light is constant—"

"Yes, Micky, even if the speed of light is constant, there are still several ways to explain how light could arrive here in less than six thousand years. One theory, built on Einstein's general theory of relativity, is based on the fact that time itself is affected by gravity. The Bible says several times that God 'stretched out the heavens.' This means the universe was originally much smaller. So it is possible that time could have moved at normal speed here on Earth, but traveled much faster in other places."

Obviously flustered, Micky stood and started pacing. "Wait, are you being serious?"

"Absolutely. That's just one of many possible explanations. It may one day be proven wrong, but that doesn't mean that we won't ever figure it out. Besides, people who believe in the big bang have a very similar problem. It's known as the 'Horizon

Problem,' so they really can't use the starlight issue as an argument against the Bible without undermining their own view."

Izzy scratched his chin. "Hmm, I read about the Horizon Problem, but never thought about it like that."

"But...but..." Micky sighed and then sat down. "Never mind."

Jonas looked at JT. "So, why were you guys arguing about the constellations in the first place?"

The four teens exchanged glances and Jax spoke. "We can't really say. It's top secret."

"Top secret?" He laughed. "Did you guys invent a time machine or something?"

That brought nervous laughter from each of the students. Jax looked at Izzy. "Should we tell him?"

"Only if he promises not to tell anyone."

"Yeah, you can't tell anyone," Micky said.

"Okay, I won't tell anyone. What's the big secret?"

"Well, you guessed it," Jax said. "We did build a time machine."

Jonas fumbled the pen he was fiddling with. "What?"

JT smiled and nodded. "Uh-huh."

His jaw dropped open. "Wait. You mean you made a time machine that actually works?"

"It works well enough to get chased by a dinosaur. I can tell you that much," Izzy said.

"Are you kidding me?" Jonas stood and pressed both hands to his head.

"No, they're serious, Mr. Ellis," JT said. "We all went back forty-five hundred years ago and Jax and Izzy were chased by what we think was an allosaurus."

"Really? That's amazing. You have to tell me the whole story."

SEVEN

"And I'll have the Gigabyte combo with a large root beer and fries," Jax told the waitress at Bits & Bytes, who scribbled down the group's order.

"Will that be everything?" she asked.

"I think so," he said, and Izzy, JT, and Micky nodded their approval.

"Alright, that will be right up."

"It's good to see that you got your appetite back," Izzy told Jax.

"Hey, I'm a growing boy," he said. He looked at JT. "I forgot to thank you for taking us to meet Jonas. It's awesome to meet someone that I have looked up to for so long."

"Yeah, thanks, girl," Micky said. "I'm gonna have to go with you to more places. We keep seeing all those cute guys."

"I think he's a bit too old for you," JT said.

"Maybe I'll just have to look him up in a couple of years to see if he's still single."

"Don't you think about anything else besides boys?" Izzy asked.

"Once in a while. But we're finally done with that science fair project, so I figured I can focus my attention elsewhere."

"Well, how about we focus on our trip for next Saturday?" Jax said as he pulled out a notebook he had carried in with him. He tugged the pen out of the spiral binding, opened the notebook, and drew a line down the middle of the page he had turned to. "Alright, the predictions for the biblical view will go on the left. The evolutionary predictions will go on the right."

Izzy spoke first. "I think the most obvious one is that the biblical view would expect to find dinosaurs and people in the same time period. The evolutionary view, of course, would not."

"Good. That's one." Jax said as he wrote it down. "What else?"

"I think the point would be the same if we found any animal that has allegedly been extinct for millions of years living at the same time as people. It wouldn't have to just be dinosaurs," JT said.

"That's true. Let me add that to the list."

"What about mammals?" Izzy asked. "I suppose the biblical model would claim that all the mammals were made on the sixth day, right?"

JT thought for a minute before responding. "Well, not exactly. I would say that all the land animals were made on day six, but water mammals, like dolphins, would have been made on the fifth day."

"Oh, right. I guess I was just thinking about land mammals. Then that's one difference we could put down. The evolutionary view teaches that only small mammals existed at the time of the dinosaurs. All the larger ones came about later. The biblical view has small and large mammals made on the same day as dinosaurs."

Jax started scribbling notes again. "So, we're saying that if we see any large mammals, then that supports the biblical view, right?"

"That sounds good," JT said. "Actually, I think we should check the time periods that the dinosaurs we saw allegedly lived. You said that you thought the one that chased you guys was an allosaurus. Well, according to evolutionists, the allosaurus lived in the late Jurassic—approximately one hundred and fifty million years ago. That's eighty million years earlier than you thought we were."

"Well, maybe it wasn't an allosaurus," Micky said.

"Yeah, it's not like you can expect us to be experts in recognizing dinosaurs," Izzy added.

"No, I agree. It may not have been an allosaurus. There are plenty of other dinosaurs that looked like that. All I'm saying is that we should try to determine whether or not the creatures we see actually line up with the evolutionary timeline."

"That's a good point, too." Jax said. "I've got a dinosaur book at home that provides all those details. I'll just take it along with us."

As he finished speaking, the waitress came up to the table carrying a tray laden with food. She gave the teens their order and they dug in.

They continued talking in between bites, and Jax added a few more predictions to the lists.

As they were finishing their lunches, Jax decided it was time to change the subject. He couldn't shake Izzy's comment about JT being intolerant.

"JT, I've been thinking about this for a couple days, and I was wondering how you would respond. What would you say to somebody who thinks that Christians are intolerant?" As he said the words, he lightly kicked Izzy's leg under the table to make sure he was paying attention.

JT finished her bite. "I guess I would agree with them. Christians are intolerant."

"Wait, did you just admit that you were intolerant?" Micky asked.

"Well, it depends on how you use the word," she said. "You see, tolerance used to refer to the idea that you put up with people that you don't agree with." She looked right at Micky. "For example, I could tolerate the fact that you don't share my faith in God. I can still love you and treat you with respect and dignity. But I don't have to agree with you on everything."

"Yeah, but that's not what I meant," Jax said.

"I know what you meant. Christians are often accused of being intolerant and like I said, we are—at least in one sense. Jesus said that He is the only way to God. If you don't trust in Him, then you won't go to heaven when you die."

Izzy sat up straight. "Can't you see how intolerant that is?"

"Well, in the true definition of the word, that's not intolerant at all. It would be better to use the word *exclusive*. That's different from the real meaning of intolerance. But if you want to use the politically correct definition, then I'm guilty." She paused and scratched her head. "But so are all of you."

"We are not," Micky said.

"You're not? Then let me ask you a question. If you are truly 'tolerant' in the new sense of the word, then you have to admit that all beliefs or religious views are equally valid, right?"

Micky nodded. "Right."

"So do you really believe that? Do you really believe that all religions are equally valid?"

"Sure. They're all just different ways that people try to get to God."

JT raised her eyebrows. "But you believe Christianity is intolerant, right?"

"Yeah, who doesn't? You said it yourself. Only Christians go to heaven, right?"

"So is that view equally valid?" JT asked.

"What do you mean?"

"Is Christianity just as valid as, say, Buddhism or Hinduism?"

Micky appeared to be struggling to find an answer. "Well…"

"You have to say 'yes' to be consistent."

"Okay, fine. It's just as valid."

"So let me get this straight. You're saying that Christianity with one God, Hinduism with millions of gods, and atheism with no God are equally valid?"

Micky and Izzy remained silent.

JT took a sip. "Don't you see the problem? You can't tell me that all views are equally valid when they are so different and contradictory. Logically, they can't all be right. Either they are all wrong, or one is right and the rest are wrong."

Micky crossed her arms and leaned back, while Izzy looked pensive.

JT let out a deep breath and spoke quietly. "Besides, if we're supposed to be so tolerant, then how come you don't tolerate my belief that Jesus is the only way to God? Why is it okay for you to be intolerant of Christianity?"

After looking down for a few moments, Micky said, "I never really thought about it like that."

"Most people don't think about it. They just repeat what they've heard other people say. That's one of the cool things that Pastor Rich has been teaching us at youth group. Not only does he try to answer all the questions that we have, but he tries to prepare us to be able to give reasons for what we believe."

"Yeah, he seemed a lot smarter than I expected," Izzy said.

JT chuckled. "Why? What did you expect?"

"I don't know. I don't remember much from when I used to go to church, but I remember thinking it was really boring. I never thought that pastors would get into subjects like that."

"Well, as far as I know, many of them don't, but I'm glad you have a different perspective on church now."

"Oh, speaking of church," Izzy said. "Jax, what were you talking to Pastor Rich about after youth group for so long?"

Jax was sort of hoping that the subject didn't come up. He wasn't quite sure how to tell Izzy that he had become a Christian, especially since Izzy had listened to several of his rants against God. Still, he didn't want to let JT down. She knew the truth. Even more importantly, he didn't want to let God down. After fumbling for a place to start, he said, "Well, I had a bunch of questions for him."

"Like what?"

"I wanted to know about pain and suffering, the age of the earth, and all that stuff. But, in the end, we didn't really focus on those things. I kept thinking about what he said about Jesus rising from the dead." His voice grew stronger and the words came easier. "I never gave it much thought before, but I couldn't deny what he said about the Resurrection. I realized that I needed Jesus in my life, so Pastor Rich explained to me how to become a Christian."

His comments were followed by an awkward silence. Jax looked at JT. She was smiling from ear to ear. He hesitated before looking at Izzy.

Izzy slowly shook his head. "Are you serious?"

Jax held Izzy's gaze and smiled. "Yeah, I'm serious." He glanced away. "I mean, I still don't have answers to all of my questions, but I know beyond any shadow of a doubt that Jesus died for my sins and rose from the dead."

Izzy closed his eyes and massaged his temples.

"Anyone want dessert?" the waitress asked.

EIGHT

"My mom said it was fine if I stayed for a while," Jax said after JT opened the front door.

"Cool. Come on in."

"Hey, Jax. It's good to see you." Mr. Bankers stood up and walked across the living room.

"Oh hi, Mr. Bankers. It's good to see you, too," Jax said. He reached out and shook Mr. Bankers hand. *Ouch. I like my knuckles where they are.*

"JT said that the meeting with Mr. Ellis this morning went really well."

"Yeah, it was sweet. You should have seen it."

"She also said that you became a believer."

"Yeah, that's true." Jax looked away. "I guess it was time for me to stop running from God. I'm just glad He was still willing to forgive me."

Mr. Bankers clapped Jax on the back. "I think we could all say the same thing. God's love is truly amazing." After a momentary silence Mr. Bankers said, "Can I get you anything to drink?"

"No thanks. I'm good."

"Okay, well, why don't you kids have a seat?"

He returned to his recliner. Jax sat down on the couch. As JT joined him, she said, "I hope you don't mind, but I asked my dad to help answer your question about why God would allow death and suffering."

Jax masked his disappointment and glanced at her dad's imposing frame. He really liked talking to just JT, but he realized that her dad had a lot more experience answering questions. Despite his size, he had a very gentle spirit. "No, that's fine with me."

"Well, alright then. JT told me that you've been upset with God for what happened to your dad."

"Yeah, ever since the accident, I've really been angry with God. I never understood how an all-powerful and all-loving God would allow something like that to happen. I still don't understand it, but I would say that I'm not angry with God anymore—not since Wednesday."

Mr. Bankers took a deep breath before starting. He scooted up toward the front of his recliner, leaned forward slightly, and looked directly at Jax as he spoke. "First of all, you know that we're all very sad about what happened to your dad. I know how tough it is to grow up without a father."

Jax's eyebrows rose, and he looked at JT.

She said, "My grandpa died in an accident when my dad was really young."

"I didn't know that. I'm sorry."

"Thanks, Jax," Mr. Bankers said. "You know, I struggled through a lot of the same feelings, but ultimately God gave me peace. JT told me about some of your conversations. She said that she stressed that God created a perfect world with no death, suffering, or disease. Well, recognizing that truth is the key to understanding the whole problem of suffering. If you don't trust what God says in Genesis, then you can't answer the problem of suffering."

"What do you mean?"

"When your dad died, how many times did you have Christians tell you something like this: 'We don't know why God lets these things happen'?"

Jax thought for few seconds before answering. "Quite a few."

"I'll bet that's one of the reasons why you have been so upset with God."

"Why? I still don't really understand what this has to do with it."

"Let me see if this helps. There are a lot of Christians who have been led to believe that the earth is billions of years old, and they try to reinterpret the first chapter of Genesis to accommodate all those years. They have come up with all sorts of theories to try to explain how we don't have to believe the plain meaning of the text."

"Are you talking about things like the Day-Age Theory?"

"Exactly."

Jax turned to JT. "I just read about that in the notes of my study Bible. I started reading Genesis the other night after I got home."

JT shook her head. "We've got one that says

that too. But just remember that only the text itself is inspired by God. The notes aren't."

"That's right," Mr. Bankers said. "Genesis is a great place to start, but, sadly, too many Christians have compromised the very first chapter of the Bible. The people who promote the Day-Age Theory, the Gap Theory, Progressive Creationism, or any of the other views like these think that they are harmonizing the Bible with billions of years. However, they end up creating more problems than they allegedly solve."

He grabbed his Bible and opened it. "Think about it. Right here, at the end of the first chapter, God looked at everything He had made, and it was 'very good.' If any of those other views is correct, then you would have death, disease, and suffering occurring for millions of years before God said everything was 'very good.'"

Jax frowned as the connection dawned on him. "But doesn't the Bible say that those things came as a result of Adam and Eve eating that fruit?"

Mr. Bankers pointed at Jax. "Precisely. You can't have it both ways. Either death and suffering are a part of God's original creation, or they are here because of man's sin. If they are part of the original creation, then God must think those things are 'very good,' which, of course, is not how He is described in the Bible. This would leave us no answer to the problem of suffering except to say that God thinks it's very good.

"On the other hand, if we just take God at His word, then death and suffering are man's fault—not God's. We brought sin, death, suffering, and disease into the world; therefore, we are to blame."

Jax cocked his head to the side. "So are you saying that my dad's death was his fault because he was a sinner?"

"Well, yes and no. Since your dad was a sinner, he deserved to die—and so do we because we're all sinners. But it's not necessarily true that your dad committed one particular sin that led to his death. Jesus talked about a tower that fell and killed eighteen people. He said that they weren't worse sinners than anyone else.

"You see, we're all sinners, living in a sin-cursed world. Since that's the case, then you can expect that good things and bad things will happen to 'good' people and 'bad' people. There's still a remnant of beauty in this world, but we have to recognize that the way the world is now is not the way God made it.

"The Bible doesn't stop there. It also provides us with the only solution to the problem of evil and suffering." He turned to another page in the Bible. "First Corinthians 15:26 says that death is the last enemy that will be destroyed. Later, in Revelation, God tells us that one day all believers will live with Him in a new heaven and a new earth, and there will be no more pain, sorrow, or suffering."

Jax nodded thoughtfully. "Mr. Bankers, I think that makes perfect sense if, and only if, Genesis is true. We've learned so many things in school that contradict what the Bible says, so how can that be the answer?"

"Jax, didn't you listen to what Mr. Ellis was saying today?" JT asked.

"I did, but he's an astrophysicist. He might be able to provide some answers in his area of study, but what about all the biologists, geologists, and paleontologists? There's just too much evidence out there that goes against what Genesis says."

"He talked about that, too." JT shifted on the couch, pulling one foot under her so she could face him more directly. "Remember, he said that he doesn't reject any of the evidence. He just interprets it through a biblical worldview rather than an evolutionary mindset. In fact, the example he gave us was from geology—the Grand Canyon."

Before Jax could reply, Mr. Bankers picked up where his daughter had left off. "It's important to understand that all facts have to be interpreted. The Grand Canyon doesn't come with a sign on it that says how old it is. By the way, you might be interested to know that in the past few decades, many scientists have moved the age of the canyon from six million to sixty million years. That's just one of thousands of examples of how scientific opinion changes all the time."

"But those dates are still way beyond the biblical timescale," Jax said.

"That's true. It just goes to show you that the things evolutionists say are facts today are completely changed tomorrow. The Bible doesn't do that. It is God's unchanging Word and can be trusted from beginning to end. Ultimately, it comes down to a matter of authority. Where are you placing your faith? Is it in the words of men, whose opinions change all the time? Or is it in the unchanging Word of the God who made everything and told us how He did it?"

Jax seriously considered Mr. Bankers' words. *How can all my science teachers be wrong? There's just—*

Mr. Bankers leaned back and crossed one leg over the other. "You guys have studied a lot of science in the past few years, but have you talked much about the philosophy of science?"

"You mean, like how science works?"

He paused and looked at the ceiling momentarily. "Well, sort of. I guess I mean how science works, but also how it doesn't work."

Jax looked up from the thread he'd been working out of the seam of his jeans. "What do you mean?"

"Well, what types of things can science really

examine? What are its limitations? What are some of the assumptions that they don't tell you about?"

"No, we really haven't talked about it." Jax scrunched up his face. "What limitations and assumptions?"

"Think about it. Science is based on the idea that we observe something, form hypotheses, and subject those hypotheses to a series of rigorous tests, right?"

"Right," Jax agreed, unsure of where the discussion was headed.

"Well, if that's true, then how can secular scientists make some of the bold claims about the past that they do? Like when they say they know that one type of animal slowly evolved into another type of animal. They weren't there to observe it, and there is no evidence for it today, but we're told that it did happen. All they have as evidence in many of these cases are just a few bone fragments. The majority of their evidence is artwork."

"Wait, are you saying—"

Mr. Bankers held up a hand. "Hold on. Let me finish. You have to recognize that there's a big difference between what we could call 'operational science' and 'origins science.' Operational science is made up of things that you can see and test in the present. Origins science covers things that have taken place in the past, and we are making educated guesses about what happened. There's a huge difference, but most science courses will never talk about it."

"So you're saying that there's a big difference between a chemistry experiment, which would be operational science, and a fossil dig, which would be origins science?" Jax asked.

"Well, close. I wouldn't say that the fossil dig itself is an example of origins science. The dig would be operational science. The scientists are using their knowledge and skill in the present to dig up something that they can observe – in the present. Now, let's say they were digging up a dinosaur skeleton. They start speculating when they tell you that the dinosaur lived sixty-five million years ago, how it hunted, or how it raised its young. That's when they make a jump to origins science. They're giving you an educated guess filled with numerous assumptions."

Jax really wanted to believe what Mr. Bankers was telling him, but he struggled to see how he could throw out years of teaching on evolution from some of the country's top teachers. "Look, I admit that what you're saying is compelling. I want to believe it, but I just don't know if I can right now. It's a lot to think through."

"Alright, I can respect that." He slapped Jax's knee as he stood up. "Just keep searching for the truth and seriously consider what God has said about the issues."

"I will."

"Well, I'd better get out and mow that yard before dinner. Jax, did you want to stay for supper?"

Jax immediately thought of the one pound hamburger he had polished off just over an hour ago. "Thanks, but I don't think I could eat anything. I just had the Gigabyte a little while ago."

Mr. Bankers laughed as he exited the room.

Jax looked at JT. "Thanks for asking your dad to talk to me. That really helped."

As JT walked him to the door, she nudged him with her elbow. "You see, I told you the Bible could answer your questions."

NINE

To our junior year," Micky said as she held up her glass of diet soda toward the middle of the table.

Jax lifted his drink. "And to our two week break before summer classes."

Izzy and JT raised their drinks and said in stereo, "To our junior year."

Jax looked around his favorite restaurant and spotted several classmates also celebrating the end of the school year, though no one sat nearby. "So are you guys all set for tomorrow?"

"Yep," Micky said. "We're meeting at your place at 7:00, right?"

"Yeah. That gives us a good fourteen to fifteen hours to explore. I made sure to fully charge the battery, so we can use your devices for a while. Plus, we'll keep the solar panels out while we're traveling. That should help sustain some of the power being used."

Izzy dug into his hot fudge sundae. "Good. I don't want to run into any of our large friends while we're there."

JT sat silent, picking at her own ice cream.

Micky waved her hand in front of JT's face. "Hello. Anybody home?"

JT jolted and quickly raised her eyes to look at Micky.

"Are you alright, girl?"

"I'm fine. I was just thinking about a couple of things for tomorrow."

"Like what?"

"Well…" JT ran her fingers through her hair. "First, we've been having a lot of debates about the biblical and evolutionary views. I just want to make sure that whatever happens tomorrow, that we stay close friends. This year has been the best year of my life, and you guys have been a huge part of it. I don't want to lose that."

Micky put an arm around her and gave her a squeeze. "Hey, don't worry about it. I'm sure you won't get too upset when we're proven right. Besides, you have to forgive us right?" she said with enough sarcasm to show she was joking.

JT pushed her away and smiled. "The real question is how are you guys going to handle it when you see that the Bible's right." She paused. "The other thing is that I had an idea about the machine itself."

"What about it?" Izzy asked.

"Well, Jax told us that you guys originally tried going back seventy million years and it didn't work, right?"

Jax nodded and looked at Izzy, who replied in the affirmative.

"So then the next day you tried forty-five hundred years ago, and then it worked, right?" JT asked.

"Yeah, that's right," Izzy said.

"So what changes did you guys make to the machine between those two attempts?"

"We didn't do anything to it. We double-checked the wiring and the programming, but we didn't change anything. Why?"

"Well, I was thinking." JT glanced around the table. "What if the reason that it didn't work the first night was that it can't go back seventy million years because there never was such a time? And maybe you really were in Egypt, or at least the coordinates were right. But according to the Bible, forty-five hundred years ago would put you before the Flood. So the world would have been much different than you expected."

Izzy scratched his head. "I don't know. I'm quite sure there's a perfectly legitimate explanation for what happened and didn't happen. Maybe we tightened a screw that needed tightening and that made all the difference."

"Maybe. But we could always try it again tomorrow now that we know the machine works."

"That's fine, but it still won't really prove anything one way or the other," Izzy said.

"Why not?"

"Well," Izzy gestured with his hands. "Let's say it doesn't work at seventy million years, I could just argue that the Space-Time Generator isn't calibrated properly. If it does work, then you could use the same argument."

"Yeah, but it worked perfectly for your last trip, didn't it? If we had a larger sample size of measurable dates—dates in history that we knew were accurate—then we could assume the machine is working properly.

"True." Izzy rubbed his chin. "I agree that we need more sample dates to know how accurate it is." He looked at Jax. "Maybe we'll have some time this summer to put these ideas to the test."

Jax looked out the living room window to see his friends walking to the front door with their arms full of supplies. He quietly hustled out to meet them. "Hey, guys. Right on time. We need to keep it down, though, because my mom is still sleeping." He led his friends into the garage. "Did you remember everything?"

"I think so," Izzy said. "I brought food and a notebook to keep track of what we see and do. Plus, I put a first-aid kit in my backpack. Micky brought some flashlights and an air horn—"

"An air horn?" Jax raised an eyebrow.

"We thought it might come in handy in case of an emergency. You know, to scare something away?"

"Oh yeah, that might work."

"And I brought the drinks," JT said.

"Alright, I've got some tools in case we need to make repairs. I also have our lists of predictions from the other day, and I loaded some basic survival gear in my backpack. Should we get going?"

"Let's do it," Izzy said. They loaded the rest of their supplies into the trunk and back seat of the car.

Once they were settled into their seats, Jax said, "So we'll try seventy million years ago first. Izzy, go ahead and program that."

Izzy clicked away on the keyboard for a few moments then glanced over his shoulder at the girls. "Everybody set? Seventy million years ago, here we come." Izzy confirmed his selection on the computer.

The countdown sequence began. "10... 9..."

Jax glanced in the rearview mirror to see that JT had her head bowed and eyes closed.

"8... 7... 6..."

"What do you think it will look like?" Micky asked.

"5... 4..."

"I have no idea, but we're about to find out," Izzy said.

"3... 2... 1."

The STG whirred into action, lights flashed all over the panel, and then... nothing happened.

Izzy seemed flustered. "Oh well, like I said last night, this test doesn't really prove anything."

"That's true," JT said. "But it certainly doesn't hurt my side of the debate."

"Alright, Izzy, let's program it to go back to one minute after we left a couple weeks ago," Jax said. "That should put us safely on the ridge, and we won't risk running into ourselves. Plus, it will be early in the morning, so we'll have a full day to explore."

Izzy turned back to the computer and made the appropriate adjustments. "Okay, we're all set."

"Hit it."

TEN

"Is this it?" Micky asked as she looked out her window.

"It looks like the same place," Jax said. "Izzy, get us hovering a little and head over there." Jax pointed to the little pathway that he and JT had walked down. "JT, our footprints should still be there, if this is the same day."

"Good thinking," she said.

Izzy soon had them hovering about five feet off the ground and moving toward the edge of the small ridge they had slept on during their previous trip. A few seconds later, Jax noticed the footprints. "There they are. Yep, it's probably the same day and just after we left since the sun is still really low in the sky."

Izzy stopped the vehicle just before it got to the edge of the ridge. "I'm going to put it down to conserve as much power as possible until we figure out where we're going."

Jax peered out the windshield. "Well, we already know what's on the ridge to the north, and we don't want any part of that. There are woods to the northwest, so that's probably not the best place for hovering."

He turned to look at the girls. "We could head out to the east and see how far this meadow goes, or we could see what's on the other side of this little ridge behind us. What do you guys think?"

"Or we could follow that river to the west. Maybe we could see those baby dinosaurs again," JT said.

"Yeah, let's follow the river," Micky said. "I want to see them too."

Izzy was looking out his window toward the east. "Why don't we do all three? How much hover time do you think we can get out of that battery?"

"I can't be completely sure. If we keep it charging while we're moving and stay about five to ten feet off the ground, then I think we can get a couple of hours before we need to set it down for a re-charge. Which reminds me, I need to put the solar panels out."

Jax popped the trunk, opened his door, and walked around to the back of the car. He pulled out the dual solar panel folder, opened it up, and slid the device into a harness he had installed on the top of the trunk. Then he grabbed a wire from the harness and plugged it into the device. As he climbed back into the car he said, "So is everyone okay with starting out to the east, and slightly north, then we'll swing around to our south and then follow the river west?"

The teens expressed their agreement, and within moments Izzy had the car hovering a few feet off the ground again. After a bumpy descent down the ridge, he soon had the car pointed in the right direction. Before long, they were traveling over the meadow.

"Okay, the battery is at about ninety-five percent. I'll keep giving you a regular update." Jax turned toward the girls and held out a notebook. "One of you wanna calculate how much time we'll have in the air?"

"Sure," Micky said as she grabbed the notebook. Using Izzy's watch to keep time, Micky asked Jax for a power level readout for each of the next five minutes.

After she finished calculating, Micky handed the notebook back to Jax. "At this rate, we've got about two and a half hours left. While you guys have been enjoying the scenery, I've been doing all the work."

"Well, there's really not much to see," Jax said. "So far it's just been this meadow."

After traveling in the same direction for another thirty minutes, Izzy took his hand off the joystick and the car slowed to a halt.

"How far do you think we've gone already?" JT asked.

Micky sat forward, looking from Jax to Izzy. "Yeah, are we there yet?"

Izzy looked at his watch and his mouth moved as if he were working the calculations in his head. After a few moments he said, "I'd guess about seven miles."

Jax opened his door, leaned over, and picked a few flowers beneath him.

"What are you doing?" Izzy asked.

Jax sat up, turned, and gave each girl a flower, filling the car with a sharp, spicy-sweet aroma. "What does it look like?"

Izzy scowled. "We talked about this before. You can't interfere with the past or you might mess things up in our time."

"Settle down, Izzy. We've already walked on the grass and that didn't change anything. I don't think picking a few flowers will hurt, either."

Izzy leaned back against the headrest for a moment and spoke quietly, as if to himself. "The time machine broke quite a few branches on that tree I was in. That didn't seem to change anything either." He faced Jax. "Let's just not get carried away."

"These are beautiful," JT said, raising her flower to her nose. "I've never seen anything like them."

"I have," Micky said. "They're all over the place. This meadow looks the same in every direction."

"Yeah, and we still haven't really found any evidence to support one view or the other," Izzy said.

"Do you think we should head south for a while and see what it looks like over there?" Jax asked.

The other three agreed, and soon they were heading south toward the river.

Ten minutes had passed before Izzy pointed

directly in front of the vehicle. "Well, that's different. It's a hill."

The time machine continued cruising at a steady pace as it climbed the hill. As they cleared the top, a massive object filled Jax's view. "Look out!"

Jax gripped the steering wheel as Izzy slammed the levels up and the car shot another twenty feet into the air.

When his stomach had returned to its customary place, Jax whistled and then looked at his friends. "Wow, that was close. What was that?"

"Hey, there's a whole herd of them," Micky said, pressing her nose against the window. "They look like a bunch of triceratopses."

"Yeah," JT said. "But they're not all the same. See, that one has one horn on its face, and there are a few of them that have a bunch of horns across the tops of their frills. They're a lot bigger than I imagined."

"There must be at least fifty of them down there." Jax reached into his backpack and pulled out his dinosaur book. After flipping through several pages, he found what he was looking for. "Look, here's a page that shows a bunch of these guys. There's got to be at least four or five different species down there."

Micky leaned forward, looked at the book Jax held open and then pointed out the window. "That one looks like a protoceratops…and that one right over there looks like a zuniceratops…and the one with all the spikes on the top of its frill, that's a styracosaurus."

The car kept hovering over the herd, and the dinosaurs didn't seem to even notice it. Izzy slowed the car down and lowered it several feet so they could spend some more time admiring the mighty beasts. After several minutes of drifting along, Jax spotted the river flowing from east to west in front of them.

"So we're going to cross the river and see what's to our south?" Jax asked.

"Yeah, I think so," Izzy said. "You guys okay with that?"

"Yep, sounds good," Micky said.

They passed over the river. The landscape on the southern side was much like that on the northern side. After traveling another ten minutes, Izzy said, "Hey, those look like fruit trees."

"Cool, let's take a closer look," Micky said.

Izzy maneuvered the vehicle in close to one of the trees. "They look sort of like apples, but not quite. I want to study some."

He nestled his side of the car up against some of the leaves and twigs so that the fruit would be reachable. He and Micky put down their windows and grabbed some of the firm red fruit. Izzy had reached back for more when a high-pitched shriek caused him to yank his hand back into the car.

Micky quickly followed suit. "What was that?"

"I'm not sure," Izzy said peering out his window. A small, furry creature came into view on the branch next to him. "It looks like a raccoon, but its body is smaller and it doesn't have the mask around its eyes."

Micky turned to JT. "Maybe it's a transitional form between some rodent and a raccoon."

JT leaned over Micky to take a closer look at the creature that still chattered at them. After a moment, she said, "Or maybe it's one of the original created kinds."

"Created kinds? Girl, what are you talking about? That's a transitional animal if I've ever seen one."

"Well, you haven't seen one because there are no such things," JT said. "You guys know all about DNA, so you should know that there is no way for a creature to get new information in its genetic code."

"We talked about all that stuff back in eighth grade biology. Miss Gonzalez showed us how it worked. Remember, natural selection and mutations?"

JT sat up straight. "Micky, it's what she didn't tell us that's really important. She didn't talk about how natural selection only works with information that is already there. It can't create new information.

"She also didn't tell us that no scientist has ever observed an example of a mutation that provided new genetic information that could turn one kind of animal into another kind. So even though we are told that natural selection and mutations are how evolution happens, they are actually the very opposite. They lead to a loss of information rather than a gain."

The little raccoon-like animal finally gave up yelling at the time machine hovering in front of it, and retreated to a different part of the tree.

"What is that 'created kind' thing you were talking about?" Izzy asked.

"Well, it's a relatively new area of research among scientists. Many creationists have called it 'baraminology' after the Hebrew words *bara* and *min*, which basically mean, 'created kind.'"

"Okay, but what is it?" Izzy asked.

"The biblical view is that God created the original kinds of animals. Later, just before the Flood, God brought two of every kind of animal to Noah so they could be kept alive on the Ark. After the Flood, the animals got off the Ark and spread throughout the world. As they scattered, the created kinds speciated, meaning that they diversified into the various species and genera we see today."

"Wait a minute," Micky said. "That's not the biblical view at all. I mean, the Flood and all that is part of the biblical view, but natural selection is an evolutionary concept."

Jax quietly watched the debate through the rear-view mirror. Since he wasn't quite sure about where he stood on the issues, he decided to stay out of the discussion if possible.

"Actually, natural selection is the opposite of evolution since, like I said before, it only works on information that is already present. Besides, natural selection is a real scientific concept. It's something we observe in the present."

"But don't creationists say that God created all the animals in their present form?" Izzy asked.

JT shook her head. "Informed creationists don't say that. Some Christians have made that claim in the past, and it's kind of turned into a stereotype that won't go away. It doesn't help that so many people continue to repeat that misinformation."

"So you're saying that creationists believe in natural selection?" Izzy asked.

"Yeah, of course we do. It's real science. I would say that God created each of the different kinds of animals with a large amount of variability in their DNA so they could adapt to numerous environments. For example, God created the original dog kind, but over the years they have adapted through natural and artificial selection to all the species and breeds we see today. There are wolves, coyotes, huskies, and poodles, but they are still dogs."

"How do you know all of this?" Micky asked. "It's not in any of our science books."

"My dad has me read other books throughout the year to counter the evolutionary teaching we receive at school. Creationism is one of his specialties, so we talk about it a lot."

Jax grabbed one of the apple-like fruits from Izzy and stared carefully as he twirled it. "It looks like it's a tie so far."

"No, it's not a tie, Jax," JT said. "Izzy, when did fruit trees allegedly evolve? Was it around the time of the dinosaurs or much later?"

Jax handed the fruit back to Izzy and raised his eyebrows.

Izzy paused for a few seconds and looked down. "Way later," he said sheepishly.

"What?" Micky said.

"And what about all those triceratops-like dinosaurs? Jax, check the timelines in your book. Evolutionists claim that those things evolved in a sequence. You know, one led to the evolution of the next. But we just saw them all at the same time. So is the evolutionary story right on this point or not?"

Jax opened the book and checked the dates under each dinosaur. "She's right."

After a few seconds of dead air, JT said, "What about all the different grasses and flowers that we've seen all morning? Our textbooks claim that they didn't evolve until long after the dinosaurs went extinct."

"Okay, I get the point," Izzy said, clearly frustrated.

"Well, maybe dinosaurs didn't die out sixty-five million years ago," Micky said. "What if we're only about ten million years ago, and a small population of dinosaurs survived the extinction event?"

"Well, either way, your position is starting to look weaker and weaker."

"Whatever."

"Okay, so maybe it's not a tie anymore," Jax said.

"Shut up, Jax." Micky said.

"Hey, take it easy. It's nothing to get upset over," Jax said. "Why don't we go explore the other direction from our entry point?"

ELEVEN

"While the battery is charging, do you guys want to check out that cave we saw back there?" Micky asked.

"I don't think we should wander from the car," Jax said as he set down his drink. He closed his eyes, breathed deeply, and listened to the rippling water. "Besides, I like it here."

"We don't have to go far, but there might be a lot of things we can see on foot that we would miss in the car."

"Micky, I hate to keep bringing this up, but we still aren't too far from our friend Al," Izzy said.

Micky tilted her head and placed both hands over her heart. "Ah, how cute. You named your pet allosaurus. Come on, we're on the other side of the river. And you guys know that predators have large territories, so there probably aren't any others around here."

"I know that," Izzy said. "But why were there two of them?"

"Since one was smaller, maybe it was young, or maybe they were male and female," Micky said.

JT stood up. "You guys can stay here then. We'll be back soon. Come on, Micky."

The girls turned and started downstream. Jax yawned and looked at Izzy, who shook his head. "Let's go, Iz. We can't let them go off on their own."

Izzy sighed. "Fine. I wish Al had chased Micky. Then we'd see how brave she is." They laughed and ran after the girls.

They walked for nearly half a mile before Jax heard a loud rumbling sound ahead. Everyone froze for a moment until Izzy said, "It sounds like a waterfall."

They continued walking. After moving beyond a slight bend in the river, Micky started running. "Wow, check it out."

Jax and the others followed. "You were right, Izzy. It is a waterfall," Jax said, as they stopped about ten feet from the edge.

They gazed in wonder at the sight in front of them. The falls dropped about eighty feet into a canyon, and from there the river continued westward as far as the eye could see. The sun was high in the sky, making the water sparkle and forming several rainbows in the mist beneath them. The spray left a cool dew on Jax's face.

"Have you ever seen anything so beautiful?" JT asked. "Too bad we agreed not to take any pictures."

"Yeah, Izzy, why did you and Jax make that rule?"

"Because if the pictures fell into the wrong hands, it could lead someone back to the time machine."

JT shoved her hands into her pockets. "I know,

but this would make one awesome picture."

Still unwilling to drop his guard, Jax turned around to make sure they were still safe. Something caught his eye at the edge of the water. "What do you suppose…?" he asked himself as he started back upstream.

"What is it?" JT asked. "What are you looking at?"

"There. Right by the bank—that little animal."

"Oh yeah, it must have come from the woods."

"It looks kind of like a possum, only it's a lot cuter," Jax said.

"It looks so cuddly. Can we keep it?" She laughed.

They moved in for a closer look and were only a few feet away when it noticed them. It stopped drinking, jerked its head toward them, and hissed.

JT screamed and took a step back. As she planted her left foot on the very edge of the bank, the ground underneath it gave way. Jax grabbed for her as she tumbled into the river, but his hands clasped only empty air. Immediately the raging current pulled her under and downstream.

Jax dove through the air and just before the river closed over him he heard JT scream, "Help!" When he surfaced, he blinked water from his eyes, desperately searching for a glimpse of her. *There. I can reach her!*

A few feet away, she struggled against the flow.

137

He lunged forward and within seconds grabbed her arm. "Gotcha!"

He turned around, but the current was now dragging both of them toward the edge of the falls. He strained against it, but to no avail. The water swept his legs out from under him as he tried to stand up, and they lost a few more precious feet.

"Jax!" Izzy yelled. "Grab this! Hurry!"

He turned and saw Izzy holding out a long branch toward him and JT. Glancing back, he realized the drop off was only about fifteen feet away and getting closer by the second. His only chance was to push as hard as he could toward the bank, even if it meant they would get closer to the falls. He wrenched his body through the water with all his might. JT maintained a death grip on his arm with one hand and swam furiously with the other.

"Hurry, Jax! Grab it!" Micky shouted.

Izzy leaned over the edge of the bank as Micky pulled back on his backpack with all her weight to keep him from falling in too.

Jax's muscles screamed as he strained for the branch. *I can make it!* It was almost in reach, and he yelled to JT, "Swim!"

Together they surged toward Izzy and his life-saving branch. Jax extended his right hand to grab the end of it. He closed his fingers around the very tip of the wood. *Got it!* But no sooner had the thought of safety popped into his mind, than he felt himself being yanked backward. The branch slipped from his hand.

"Jax! JT!" Micky and Izzy screamed. Izzy stared in horror at the churning, empty white water. Over the sound of the crashing falls, he heard two distinct screams, quickly snuffed out by the torrent around them.

Micky took a couple of steps backward and slumped to the ground, sobbing.

Izzy couldn't think. *It's a dream. I'm dreaming.* But the water on his face, the rushing sound in his ears—it was all real.

After a few seconds, he shook his head, forcing himself to move. "We have to see if they made it." He cautiously moved closer to the edge of the falls and peered over.

"Can you see them?" Micky's voice trembled, barely rising above the noise around them.

"No. All I can see is the water." He continued scanning the scene far beneath him, but saw nothing except the waterfall and the billows of spray issuing from it. After losing all hope of seeing any sign of life, he walked back toward Micky with his shoulders slumped and head down.

She stood up, and Izzy tried to console her with a hug. "We have to go look for them," he said. "You guys came back for me. There's no way we aren't going to look for them."

Between sobs and sniffles, she said, "Let's get back to the car."

"That won't do any good. It's gotta be at least eighty feet down. There's no way we can compensate for that large of a drop. We'll end up falling half that distance—even with the hover technology. There's no way down from here so we'll have to keep walking to see if we can find a way down."

Micky looked over to the edge of the falls. "It looks like we might have to walk quite a ways to get down."

"We'll walk however long it takes. If there's any chance that they're alive, we have to get to them." He felt better saying the words, as if by sheer determination he could will Jax and JT to survive.

They made their way into the trees to their left and had to walk south from the falls for about a hundred yards before they could finally continue moving west. After several minutes, the forest noises replaced the sound of the waterfall.

Traveling through the thick woods was hard work and time consuming. After walking along the top of the canyon for nearly an hour, they finally came to a place where the undergrowth was thinner, the trees farther apart. "Well, I still don't see a way down, but at least we can move a little quicker," Izzy said.

After a couple more minutes, Micky stopped

140

and pointed. "What's that?"

"What's wh—" Izzy followed her finger. "It looks like smoke. Is it a forest fire?" *That's just what we need.* He could see a thick black plume rising from behind a hill in front of them, but could not see the cause of it.

"I don't know. Let's go check it out."

They dashed forward and started up the small hill. When they were about five feet from the top, Izzy looked ahead toward the source of the smoke. *What in the world?*

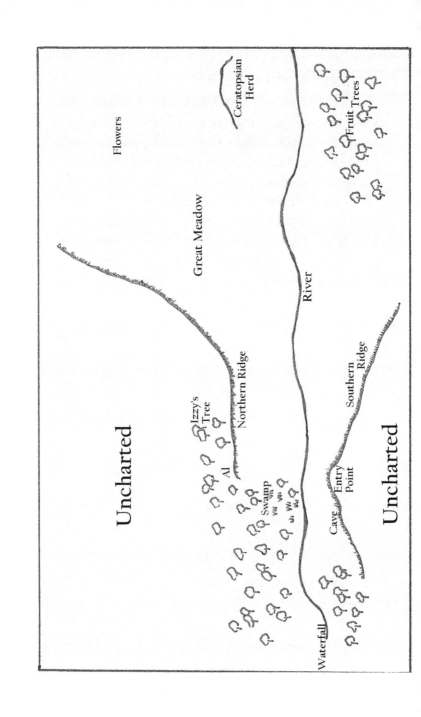

Epilogue

Ellen Thompson looked out the living room window in time to see a black sedan pull into the driveway. When two men exited the vehicle, her heart sank. It was Agent Kimball and his partner, Agent Johnson. *I can't do this again.* She bit her lip as tears built up at the corners of her eyes. With as much resolve as she could muster, she met the men at the door.

"Sorry to disturb you, Mrs. Thompson," Agent Kimball said. "But we have news for you that we thought would best be delivered in person. May we come in?"

With a slight nod, she opened the door farther and allowed the men into her living room. They sat down on the sofa while she sank into the overstuffed chair and braced for the worst.

"We'll get right to the point, ma'am, and be out of your hair," Agent Johnson said. "New evidence has come to light in our investigation. The short version is that your husband is no longer a suspect."

Mrs. Thompson sat dumbfounded. "I…I'm sorry?" she asked, hoping with all her might that she had heard correctly.

"We've cleared your husband's name in this case. Someone sent us a video taken the night of the accident that clearly shows a group of known terrorists infiltrating the lab. We're currently working with all of the intelligence and security organizations in the country to determine just who it was that did this."

She wiped a tear from her eye and smiled. "You don't know how happy I am to hear that. Thank you. I never doubted my husband. I know you were just doing your job, but it was killing me to hear him implicated."

Agent Kimball stood, signaling Agent Johnson to rise as well. Mrs. Thompson also left her seat and escorted the men back to the door.

"Thank you again for your time, Mrs. Thompson," Agent Kimball said as he shook her hand. "We're sorry we caused you so much trouble. Don't worry, we'll find those really responsible and bring them to justice."

She could only nod her head again and then shut the door behind the men. Slowly, she returned to the living room and collapsed in the chair. She cried a little, mostly out of joy, then reached for the phone to call Jax.

Immediately, she heard a message she never expected to hear. "We're sorry, the number you have dialed is out of network. If you'd like to leave a brief message, it will be received as soon as the customer returns to an area of coverage."

She glanced at her phone to verify that she'd dialed the right number. *His phone shouldn't be out of signal range anywhere within driving distance.* After hanging up and trying again, she left a brief message.

"Jax, it's your mother. Call me as soon as you get this. I have wonderful news about your father."

THANKS

The authors would like to thank all the people who helped make this series a reality. For their creative input and support, we thank Casey, Abigail, Kayla, Nick, Keith, John, Jevon, Kian, Roger, and Gary.

We want to say a very special thank you to Reagen Reed for her invaluable assistance in editing the series and forcing us to be better writers.

We extend an extra special thank you to Melissa Mathis (a.k.a. Inkhana) for her incredible artwork. Thank you for using your talents for our Lord and Savior Jesus Christ and for your efforts to glorify Him through the use of Manga. If you like the illustrations in this series please visit Melissa's website at www.christianmanga.com and be sure to check out her books.

Finally, we thank Jesus Christ for loving us so much that He willingly died in our place and saved us from our sins. Without Him nothing is possible.

the Authors

Tim Chaffey is a husband, father, pastor, teacher, cancer survivor, author, and apologist, with a passion for reaching young people with the gospel. He earned a B.S. and M.A. in Biblical and Theological Studies, a Master of Divinity specializing in Apologetics and Theology, and a Th.M. in Church History and Theology.

Tim is the content manager for the Ark Encounter and Creation Museum. He is also the founder of Risen Ministries, which is home to his blog, podcast, and speaking ministry. He has written over a dozen books, including *The Remnant Trilogy* and *In Defense of Easter: Answering Critical Challenges to the Resurrection of Jesus.*

Joe Westbrook is a husband, father, occasional writer and blogger, aspiring theologian, and amateur woodworker. He pays the bills by working in a hospital lab, though he has ambitions to find a creative career that can be accomplished out of his home.

Joe lives in central Iowa. You can follow his exploits on Facebook by searching for Central Iowa Craftsman, Central Iowa Theologian, or Joe Westbrook Author.

Made in the USA
Coppell, TX
09 July 2020

30438689R00085